DAUGHTER OF MY PEOPLE

HENRIETTA SZOLD AND HADASSAH

JEWISH BIOGRAPHY SERIES

DAUGHTER OF MY PEOPLE

HENRIETTA SZOLD AND HADASSAH

Hazel Krantz

illustrated with photographs

LODESTAR BOOKS   E. P. DUTTON   NEW YORK

Photograph on page 120: Courtesy of Eva Michaelis.

All other photographs: Courtesy of the Hadassah Archives.

Library of Congress Cataloging in Publication Data

Krantz, Hazel.
    Daughter of my people.

    (Jewish biography series)
    "Lodestar books."
    Includes index.
    Summary: Traces the life of the Hadassah women's organization's first president, who dedicated its activities to improving the living conditions of Jews in Palestine.
    1. Szold, Henrietta, 1860–1945—Juvenile literature. 2. Hadassah, the Women's Zionist Organization of America—Juvenile literature. 3. Zionists—United States—Biography—Juvenile literature. [1. Szold, Henrietta, 1860–1945. 2. Hadassah, the Women's Zionist Organization of America. 3. Social workers. 4. Jews—Biography. 5. Zionists] I. Title. II. Series.
    DS151.S9K73 1987 956.94'001'0924 [B] [92] 87-8826
    ISBN 0-525-67236-2

Published in the United States by E. P. Dutton,
2 Park Avenue, New York, N.Y. 10016,
a division of NAL Penguin Inc.

Published simultaneously in Canada by
Fitzhenry & Whiteside Limited, Toronto

Editor: Virginia Buckley

Printed in the U.S.A.   COBE   First Edition
10 9 8 7 6 5 4 3 2 1

This book is dedicated to Florence Krantz,
who has devoted her life to the furtherance
of the work of Henrietta Szold.

Contents

Acknowledgments

The main source of material for this book was the collection of the letters of Henrietta Szold in the archives of Hadassah's national headquarters in New York City. The kindness and cooperation of the Director of the Archives, Dr. Lawrence D. Geller, and his assistant, Ira Daly, made it possible for me to share Miss Szold's own lively accounts of her experiences. Dr. Geller also provided me with case histories of several Youth Aliyah children. The young people mentioned in the book were real, representative of the thousands who passed through the Youth Aliyah program. Former Youth Aliyah student Joseph Mohr graciously provided firsthand information about his experiences.

Other information came from a "Report on Youth Aliyah," written in German by Eva Michaelis-Stern and published in the *Bulletin* of the Leo Baeck Institute #70, 1985, translated into English by Shoshana Poreh. Mrs. Michaelis also shared friendship and warm personal reminiscences during a lively correspondence. Emma Ehrlich, Miss Szold's personal secretary, and head of the Henrietta Szold Archives in Jerusalem, was also very helpful.

Historian Shulamit Reinharz, of Brandeis University, contributed material regarding Manya Shohat and a letter from Miss Szold to Mrs. Shohat. Dr. Michael Poreh, of the Haifa Technion, Shoshana Poreh, and Amir Poreh checked the manuscript for historical accuracy in respect to Palestine and Israel.

Out-of-print material—*Balm in Gilead, the Story of Hadassah* by Marlin Levin (Schocken Books, 1973), and *Woman of Valor, the Story of Henrietta Szold* by Irving Fineman (Simon & Schuster, 1961)—were made available to me by Mrs. Rose Matzkin, former national president of Hadassah, from her personal collection.

Information about the Tehran children was derived in part from "The Hadassah Archives: Attic in the Basement," by Lawrence D. Geller, *Hadassah Magazine*, March 1986.

And finally, I wish to express my appreciation to my first reader, my husband, Michael Krantz, whose insight and encouragement kept things going and whose protection of my time and quiet permitted the book to be written.

Hazel Krantz
Fort Collins, Colorado

DAUGHTER OF MY PEOPLE

HENRIETTA SZOLD AND HADASSAH

1

The Remarkable
Miss Szold

The train from Damascus lurched and creaked on its way to Tiberias. In the rear of the car, an Arab family noisily picnicked from a huge basket. A baby kept crying fretfully.

Leaning back against the cracked leather seat, Henrietta Szold turned her head and fondly studied her sleeping mother, Sophie Szold, widow of the eminent Rabbi Benjamin Szold of Baltimore. Little, round, and pink-faced, with a halo of white hair, Mamma had trotted all over Europe with Henrietta and now was ready to tackle the 1909 wilderness of Palestine.

The trip had been Mamma's idea. She had said to Henrietta that she wanted to visit Vienna once more and see the relatives she had left behind many years ago when she and young Rabbi Szold came to America. But Henrietta knew that Mamma's real concern had been herself. She wanted Henrietta to get away and to find some distraction from the bitter ending of her romance with Louis Ginsburg. Quite surprisingly, Henrietta's employer, the Jewish Publication

Society, had not only granted her the leave to travel but a gift of money so that she could visit the Holy Land, then called Palestine.

Restlessly, Henrietta looked out the window at the rolling landscape. The early November sunshine flooded the brown and amber land and distant craggy hills. Every so often they passed a group of white-clad Bedouin, moving slowly and silently, in time with their grazing flocks.

In spite of all she and Mamma had seen on their travels— the wonderful paintings in the galleries in England, the visit to Italy, the relatives in Vienna—the pain in Henrietta's heart had not gone away. You take your griefs with you wherever you go, she thought.

But this was nonsense. She was forty-nine years old, too old to be mooning over a lost love. And yet, she and Louis Ginsburg had shared moments so dear, intimate talks and long walks, it seemed as if they were one person. But Louis needed a wife who was younger. Abruptly, with no warning, he returned from a trip abroad and announced his engagement. Apparently, he had thought of Henrietta merely as a loving friend.

She sighed. Perhaps she had been wrong, the whole pattern of her life a mistake. The remarkable Miss Szold, the scholar who had learned languages and Jewish philosophy from her father, the clever Miss Szold, who had translated great works of literature for the Jewish Publication Society and edited the writings of scholars. But where, she thought, tears blurring the rushing landscape outside the window, is my home? Where are my children?

It was not that she had been scorned by men. She had been a beautiful little girl, born on December 21, 1860, in Baltimore, the daughter of the rabbi of Oheb Shalom Congregation. Henrietta was the oldest of six girls. One, Johanna, died in early childhood and Sadie at twenty-six. The other sisters were Rachel, the youngest, who filled the rabbi's house on Lombard Street with song and dancing; clever Adele, the

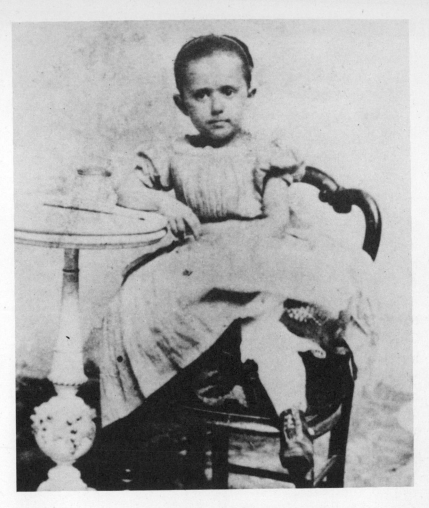

Henrietta Szold at six

rebel, now active in the new Women's Suffrage movement; and Bertha, practical and motherly. Bertha was thirteen years younger than Henrietta, but theirs was the closest bond. Bertha's children, Benjamin and Harriet, almost took the place of the children Henrietta never had.

The sisters were all married now. Rachel had gone off to Wisconsin with her psychologist husband, Joseph Jastrow. Adele and her husband, Thomas Seltzer, lived in New York, near Henrietta and her mother. Bertha and Louis Levin lived

In 1877, at seventeen

in Baltimore, but came frequently to New York to visit at the
apartment at 528 West 123rd Street, where Henrietta and her
mother had moved after Rabbi Szold's death. The apartment
was in what was then considered a fashionable neighbor-
hood, across the street from the New York office of the Jewish
Publication Society, where Henrietta worked.

In Baltimore when she was young, suitors had come calling
on Rabbi Szold's daughter Henrietta. She had lovely dark
brown hair, which she still brushed with a hundred strokes

every night, and a trim figure. Throughout her life, Henrietta took good care of her appearance. Her most beautiful features were her soft, deep brown eyes, full of understanding and wisdom, and her sweetly curving mouth.

But to the young Henrietta, there was only one man worth considering. That was her beloved father. How silly the young men who came courting seemed in comparison. And the games girls had to play, blushing and tittering, in order to keep the men interested! Henrietta thought such flirtations were a waste of time. She had more important things to do.

Rabbi Szold's wisdom and learning extended far beyond Baltimore, and he had an extensive correspondence as well as his own writings. Henrietta was his assistant. She learned from him Hebrew and fluent German, his native tongue. Most of all, she absorbed his love of God and of all living things, God's creations. Later, she went to a seminary and studied with rabbinical students, although women were not permitted at that time to become rabbis. But she wanted to understand more about the Bible and the Talmud so that she could share her father's wisdom.

When Henrietta was in her twenties, she became interested in the plight of poor Russian Jews, who were streaming into the United States, escaping from the poverty of the little villages and the cruel pogroms of the Cossacks. She taught in a Russian school, where the immigrants from Eastern Europe learned English. She loved her students and grew to understand the beauty of their language, Yiddish, and the culture from which they came. Later she was to translate some of the writings of wonderful Yiddish writers into English, and Heinrich Graetz's enormous *History of the Jews* from German into English.

As she looked out the window now at the Syrian landscape, an Arab appeared on the crest of a hill, riding a great black stallion. He sat there for a moment and then gave his steed a mighty kick and went galloping off into the desert, his white kaffiyeh headdress streaming in the wind.

Somehow, she felt she was like that unknown Arab, ready
to rush off into the wilderness on an adventure. Everything
interested her; she could not pass a plant without learning
its name and everything about it. But mostly, she had a
passion for ideas.

One of the most thrilling evenings in her life had been the
time when she heard a lecture given by a handsome young
man, exactly her age, with dark hair and a perfectly shaped
beard and eyes that held her like magnets. His name was
Theodor Herzl.

An Austrian journalist, Herzl had grown up hardly knowing that he was Jewish. He was assigned by his newspaper
to cover the celebrated Dreyfus case in France. Captain Alfred
Dreyfus had been accused of treason. As Herzl heard the
testimony, he became uneasy. It didn't seem to make sense;
there was no proof that this man had betrayed his country.

Then it occurred to him what was happening. Certain people, jealous because Dreyfus, a Jew, held an important place
in the French army, had invented the evidence. Dreyfus was
not guilty; he was the victim of anti-Semitism.

When Herzl saw the epaulets of rank stripped from Captain Dreyfus's shoulders before the captain was sent to the
terrible prison on Devil's Island, he was full of resentment
and fear.

But he soon realized that resentment and fear never ac-
complish anything. On his way back to Austria, he gathered
his thoughts and tried to find a solution. Suddenly, he had
a wild and impractical idea. When he got home he wrote a
book about it, called *The Jewish State*.

Herzl proposed that the Jewish people have a nation of
their own, where they would not have to fear anti-Semitism.
Surprisingly, other people—not all of them Jewish—had the
same idea. In England, some very religious Christians felt
that it would be right for the ancient land of Israel to belong
to the people of the Bible, the Jews.

Herzl traveled to many countries and convinced people

that Jews could have a home. They could settle in their ancient land, Palestine, which was part of the Ottoman Empire, ruled by Turkey.

Beginning in 1881 in Russia and Poland, anti-Semitism became not only uncomfortable but very frightening. Without warning, Cossacks rode into Jewish villages and burned and raped and murdered. Some Jews fled or hid, but many of them were killed.

Some young Jews heard about Herzl's idea. They said, "Why should we stay in a country where the people act like savages? We will go to Palestine and build up the land."

They called themselves the Hovevei Zion (Lovers of Zion). When they went to Palestine, they found it to be a barren place, neglected by the Arabs who lived there. Many of the settlers died from diseases like malaria. Others became discouraged by the hard life and left. But a few successful Zionist settlements grew. And there were a handful of people in other countries who felt that Zionism could succeed, although most people thought it was a pretty ridiculous idea.

The thought of the Jewish homeland filled Henrietta with excitement. Not only would this country be a refuge for persecuted Jews—she knew about their plight from stories told to her by the students at the Russian school—but it would be a noble land. It would be governed by the rules of justice and love she had learned from her father. All of these wonderful ideas about how people should treat one another would leave the dry pages of the Talmud and come to life in a real place, an example to the world.

One day she went to a meeting of an organization to which she belonged, the National Council of Jewish Women. While giving a speech to the members, she drew herself up and in an impassioned voice declared, "I am a Zionist!"

When her father died, Henrietta left Baltimore and went to work for the Jewish Publication Society as an editor. At first she was nervous, unsure of how to do editing. But Louis Levin, Bertha's husband, was a publisher and taught her the craft. As with everything she did, Henrietta devoted herself to her work with exacting care.

Henrietta was brought from reveries of the past into the present by a great noisy clashing and grinding of brakes. The train was pulling into Ramah station. Ahead of them was a wide gleam of blue water, Lake Tiberias. And on the other side of the lake was the land itself . . . Palestine!

"Mamma, Mamma." She shook the sleeping Sophie. "We're here. Wake up!"

Feverishly, she began gathering up their bundles. This was no time for old regrets. Like the Arab on the horse, it was time to gallop into adventure.

2

Hope

As a tall boatman helped Sophie over the side of his boat, which was to carry them from Ramah to Tiberias, Henrietta nodded to him. When it was her turn, his sinewy arm reached for her and he smiled, white teeth gleaming in his dark face. *"Salaam aleikim."*

"Shalom," she replied. The Arab was, after all, a kinsman, descended, like herself, from Abraham.

She belonged to a small study group of women called Hadassah, who were interested in Zionism. Henrietta, who considered herself a realist, discounted what she considered a lot of romantic nonsense the women gushed about the Holy Land. But, even so, when she stepped ashore at Tiberias, dismay hit her like a slap across the face.

It was a filthy city, a city of blackened stone buildings, of narrow, stench-filled streets, of sick and impoverished people, both Jews and Arabs. The Jews were not the bronzed pioneers imagined by the ladies of the study group. Bearded, with curled earlocks and broad-brimmed Polish hats and long caftans, they moved slowly through the city. These were the pious ones, some of them old men who had come to die in the Holy Land. They were supported by other Jews from all over the world. These objects of charity hardly looked like the builders of a Jewish state.

Henrietta and her mother climbed into a hired carriage, which took them through narrow streets to their hotel, where they left their luggage. Then they told the cab driver to take them to the Alliance Israelite School, where they were to meet a Mr. Kahane, who would be their guide, an arrangement made by Henrietta's Zionist friends.

"At least," said Henrietta, trying to sound hopeful, as they stood before the crumbling building that housed the school, "the Jews in Tiberias are not too desperate to found schools."

Ezra Kahane was a serious-looking young man in a high starched collar. He bowed ceremoniously and led the two ladies out to the teeming street for a walking tour of the city.

Henrietta grabbed Sophie by the arm as they stepped over a puddle awash with orange peels and eggshells. "Mamma, what have you got in your bag? It looks as though you've brought your lunch."

Sophie glanced at her bulging handbag and shrugged. "Nothing important. Just a few things I might need."

Mr. Kahane led them through winding cobblestone passageways past ancient decaying buildings. Arab vendors hawked everything from fly-ridden food to kaffiyehs. Carts and wagons and occasional carriages jammed the way and sent pedestrians scurrying. Over everything there lingered, stronger than all the other mingled odors, the constant ripe smell of horse manure.

Suddenly, Sophie stopped. As Henrietta and Mr. Kahane watched in amazement, she approached a little boy about eight years old, whose face was etched in dirt. Sophie opened her handbag and brought out a bar of pure castile soap she had purchased in Vienna. Then she drew out a washcloth she'd taken from the hotel.

"Mamma, don't," squealed Henrietta as the boy flinched in terror. But he didn't run away. He kept staring at the crazy old woman with the strange object in her hand.

Sophie reached into the bag once again and this time she brought out a piece of hard candy. The little boy's frightened look changed to one of delight. Eagerly, he grabbed for the candy.

"Not now," said Sophie, jerking the candy out of his reach. As he watched with wary fascination, she went over to a horse trough, turned on the water faucet, and wet the washcloth. Then she rubbed it vigorously with soap.

"Oh no," moaned Henrietta as Sophie approached the boy. Mr. Kahane just stood by, frozen in astonishment.

After a little pantomime consisting of the boy ducking his head and Sophie coming after him with the washcloth, holding the candy just out of reach, the child got the idea. Sophie applied washcloth and soap to his face and rubbed it until he yowled. When his face was a shining clean circle above his dirty neck, she gravely presented him with the candy and a coin.

She went back to the faucet, rinsed off the washcloth, and waited for the next customer. A horde of dirty little boys, seeing the candy and the coin, besieged her and she went to work, wiping and washing, and giving candy until she had to appeal to Mr. Kahane for rescue. He waded into the crowd, waving his hands, and sent the urchins scampering. Wiping perspiration from his forehead and resuming his role of dignified guide, he then continued shepherding them on their walk.

"Oh, Mamma." Henrietta laughed.

"I do not believe in just bemoaning conditions. When I see something wrong, I do something about it."

Henrietta looked at her sharply. Her mother had a way of teaching, not through a barrage of words, but by example.

As she walked, Mamma's meaning became clear. It had to

do with their old saying: "When you feel sorry for yourself, do something for somebody quick." She had been feeling rather sorry for herself lately. She reached over and clasped Sophie's shoulder to show that she understood.

A beggar woman sat with her back to the stone wall of a building, holding out a skinny, dirty hand for alms. In her lap there rested a baby, his eyes clustered with flies feeding upon oozing pus.

Putting a coin in the woman's hand, Henrietta could not help but scold, with Mr. Kahane translating into Arabic, "Why don't you brush the flies from your child's eyes?"

The woman looked at her dully and said something that the guide translated, "They'll only come back again."

Ashamed, Henrietta moved off. She had been insensitive. Indignation took hold of her. Why was it like this? Why was there so much disease and filth? Was no one interested in the health of the people, in simple public sanitation?

If she had inherited her idealism from her father, Henrietta had also inherited Sophie's practical sense. It had always been puzzling to her why people could not look at a situation, figure out what had to be done, and do it.

"What is the matter with the baby's eyes?" asked Sophie.

"Trachoma," Mr. Kahane replied. "Many children go blind."

"Are there no doctors?" Henrietta inquired.

"Certainly." Mr. Kahane pointed at an unkempt-looking man on a mule stationed in front of a pharmacy. "There's one."

As they watched, a man approached the doctor. He seemed to be complaining of head pains, for he rubbed his forehead. The doctor nodded wisely and scribbled a prescription on a piece of paper. The patient gave the doctor a coin and scurried into the pharmacy to have the prescription filled.

"This is scandalous," Henrietta exclaimed. "Are there no hospitals, with real doctors?"

"In Jerusalem there are four Jewish hospitals," Mr. Kahane assured her. "But it's not just a matter of bringing good

Sophie and Rabbi Benjamin Szold

medicine to Palestine. The people have to be ready to accept
it. You have to remember how ignorant most of them are.
They believe in folk medicine. For instance, for trachoma
they use egg yolks and a mustard plaster over the temples.''
Henrietta shuddered.

"Of course," Mr. Kahane continued, "that doesn't take away the evil eye. For that you need an amulet."

The next day Israel Shohat, husband of an old friend of Henrietta's, Manya Shohat, came to take them to see rural settlements. She had been introduced to Manya by her friend Rabbi Judah Magnes of Temple Emanuel when Manya visited the United States. A dark, stocky young Russian woman, Manya had created a solution for the new pioneers who couldn't find jobs or buy land. She had planned a collective settlement, which she called a kibbutz.

When she established the kibbutz she was unmarried. A young man, Israel Shohat, heard about Manya's experimental farm, which was to be in Sejera, a rather remote region. The kibbutz idea interested him, but not particularly as a way of supporting pioneers. Israel Shohat headed a secret organization, the Shomrim (Watchmen). Bedouin sometimes attacked Jewish settlements and the Jews couldn't depend on their Turkish rulers to defend them. Of course, training a Jewish defense corps was against the laws of Palestine. Israel felt that the kibbutz would provide an ideal shelter and cover for his operations.

Manya was agreeable. It was desirable to have defenders in their midst. The arrangement worked out well. Although the kibbutz at Sejera lasted only a year, the connection between Manya and Israel became permanent and they were married.

Henrietta wanted to know how the experiment had succeeded.

"Beyond our dreams," said Israel. "Finally we have a form of community that is successful. It's democratic. All property belongs to the whole. People are free to leave or stay. Women are the equals of men, both in their tasks and in the administration of the kibbutz. Kibbutzim are planned for Degania and Yeminah. We're on our way to Yeminah now."

As Israel Shohat's wagon trundled through barren fields glistening in a blend of colors—tawny browns, grays, and

yellows, with here and there a flash of delicate pastel wild-
flowers and the green of a wind-bent cypress—Henrietta felt
that this was indeed the Holy Land. The air seemed to vibrate
with energy. She thought of the prophets of biblical times
going into the desert and receiving the music of the universe.

With a little twinge of regret, for the land was beautiful in
its wild state, Henrietta imagined it turned into a land of
milk and honey, flourishing with abundant crops. The words
of a new song, called "Hatikvah" ("Hope"), written by the
poet Naphtali Herz Imber, ran through her head:

> Our hope is not yet lost,
> The hope of thousands of years,
> To be a free people in our land,
> In the land of Zion,
> In Jerusalem.

The wagon rumbled over stones and ruts on a road that
was merely a track through the wilderness. Israel coughed.

"Do you have a cold?" asked Sophie solicitously.

"No," he said. "A touch of tuberculosis. TB's the sickness
of the pioneer. That and malaria. The winter rains, poor
shelter, not enough to eat . . . you pay a price."

Henrietta looked at him. "I think you will overcome your
illness," she said slowly. Israel was a strong man and the
Palestine sun, which could be harsh, had the warmth needed
to burn out his illness; at that time, drugs to cure tuberculosis
had not been discovered and the treatment was rest and
sunshine. Manya had written to her about Israel's illness.
Henrietta would have to let her friend know her feeling of
optimism.

As if reading Henrietta's thoughts, Israel said, "Manya is
off on a speaking trip. She will be disappointed not to see
you."

"How is she?"

"A fountain of energy, as always, the center of wherever

she is. If all the men in my Shomrim group had her courage, the settlers would have nothing to worry about."

He pointed his whip at a cluster of black tents on the crest of a hill. Nearby, children tended sheep under the watchful eyes of their white-clad fathers. "Bedouin. They are a proud and fierce people. They have their own ways, which we respect. But they think the land is theirs. All of the land where the settlers live was purchased legally, but what do these people know about land sales? They see the Jewish settlers as taking their grazing lands from them just as the white men took the land from the American Indians."

"But I'm afraid we grabbed the Indian lands instead of buying them," said Henrietta wryly.

Israel nodded politely, not wanting to criticize Americans.

"But you have one thing in common with the American settlers. Attacks. Bedouin attacks instead of Indian raids," Henrietta remarked. "What is happening with your Shomrim?"

Israel whipped his horse smartly and the animal labored up a rutty incline. "At Sejera we worked out some of our tactics and we have a good force now. It seems that the government will give permission for the Shomrim to be a legal defense force. We will be much safer that way. The Turks rule this country, but they are no friends of the Jews. They're Moslems, after all, descendants of Ishmael. They've never forgiven us for the driving of Hagar, Sarah's handmaid in the Bible, into the wilderness with her child."

"But that happened over three thousand years ago!" Henrietta exclaimed.

"Arabs and Turks live in the past. They have grudges, terrible resentments that grow with time instead of dimming. Of course, some are good neighbors. But the tribe comes first. Their loyalty will never be to the Jews."

Henrietta recalled the Arab who had helped her into the boat at Ramah. "I think there can be a nation where the Jews

and Arabs will live in peace. They have to respect one another. Education is the way, and—and"—she searched for
a word—"neighborliness."

The horse jogged along and the wagon rumbled, seeming
as if it would burst apart at every turn of the wheel. Israel,
coughing and encouraging the horse with the whip when
necessary, patiently answered all of Henrietta's questions
about plants; she had to know the name of everything she
saw.

"If you like plants," he suggested, "you must meet Aaron
Aaronsohn, our famous agronomist. He's got an experimental station, famous for a new strain of wheat."

"There's someone else I think you'd find interesting," he
continued, "Meier Dizengoff, the planner of the new city,
Tel Aviv."

"Hill of spring," Henrietta translated.

Israel grinned. "It's being built near the sea. An all-Jewish
city."

"With plumbing and everything?" Henrietta joked.

"Plumbing, even electricity, and sewers, horsecars, and
stores." Israel looked as if he were seeing a vision of paradise.
"Tall buildings like New York, and hotels and beaches."

Henrietta laughed. "I'd like to meet this Mr. Dizengoff."

They continued along in silence. The dry air, with its hint
of coolness, triggered a cascade of thoughts in Henrietta's
brain. This country was full of creative possibilities and adventure, but there was so much to be done. She thought of
the tiny Zionist study group to which she belonged. It was
called Hadassah for two reasons. It had been founded around
Purim, the celebration of Queen Esther, whose name in Hebrew was Hadassah. Also, the mother of Emma Gottheil,
the woman who founded the study group, was named Hadassah, and Mrs. Gottheil wanted to honor her.

Suppose, thought Henrietta, instead of reading flowery
poetry about Zion and sighing over the brave pioneers, the

ladies of Hadassah did something practical, like sending medical help to those poor children with the terrible eye disease, trachoma?

But what could ten women do? She thought deeper. Why only ten women? Why not recruit more members, have chapters in other places?

Henrietta shook her head. Wild impractical ideas. This place was getting to her. But she made up her mind to pay attention to everything she saw on this trip and to make notes, so she could share her experiences with American Zionists.

The first place they visited was an agricultural colony at Yeminah, patterned after Manya Shohat's original kibbutz. The buildings at Yeminah were crude, but cotton flourished in the fields and sturdy orange trees were maturing in the orchard.

They were taken to visit the children's house, kept scrupulously clean, where children were cared for, all together, so their mothers could work. "Our finest crop," commented the children's nurse. Looking at the lively sunburned youngsters clambering all over homemade playground equipment, Henrietta and Sophie agreed.

At the corners of the settlement, tall watchtowers gleamed in the sun. Within the watchtowers, the Shomrim defense soldiers took turns with rifles ready, to protect the settlement against marauders. Others patrolled the borders of the fields, especially at night. Henrietta noted the position of the children's houses, in the center of the kibbutz. Circle the wagons, she thought, remembering how American settlers would protect their camps by parking their covered wagons in a circle.

The next day Henrietta and Sophie returned to Yeminah to Tiberias where, through contacts in the Jewish Agency, they were able to meet with Meier Dizengoff, the developer of Tel Aviv. Mr. Dizengoff, a chubby little man who reminded Henrietta of bustling realtors in Baltimore, met them in Jaffa and took them in his carriage into what seemed like a hilly desert near the Mediterranean Sea.

"Here," he said proudly, waving a pudgy hand, "is the city of Tel Aviv."

Lifting their long skirts, the women followed him down a sand-strewn road. They walked through muddy little yards and visited the inhabitants of tiny white houses smelling of wet plaster and whitewash. A proud hostess served them tea in her small sitting room, all the while bemoaning the sand that gritted her tiled floor. But everything was clean and new, and fresh healthful sea breezes came through the windows.

Afterward, they stood outside in a lane with the proud title of Herzl Street and looked at the billows of sand leading down to the turquoise crescent of the Mediterranean.

"Over there," gestured Mr. Dizengoff, "we will build an academy, the last word in modern education. And a synagogue, of course." He pointed to a bare hill on which a scrubby cypress fought the onslaught of wind. "That will be our business section . . . many shops, the most modern. And here," he turned and held out his hand grandly, "will be the best of all. Look at that wonderful view of the sea. This is where we will build splendid hotels so that our friends from America can stay. Be sure to tell them that when you return to New York."

Israel Shohat picked up the Szolds the next day and drove them to Zikhron Yaacov, a village founded by Romanians in 1882. Nearby were vineyards planted by Baron de Rothschild as part of his project to turn Palestine into a wine-producing country. In the village there were neat houses, many of them belonging to tidy German families, but Henrietta was distressed to see a public park overgrown with weeds and neglected. It troubled her when people were careless.

The pride of Zikhron Yaacov was the agricultural station run by Aaron Aaronsohn. When Henrietta met the members of the Aaronsohn family—the father (unfortunately, his wife had recently died), young Rifka, vibrant Sarah, and tall blue-eyed Aaron—she felt an immediate kinship with them.

Aaron showed the Szolds a field of wheat that had been sown with seed from a strain of wild grain he had discovered. "Wheat that grows wild here certainly should be able to succeed in this climate. We take slips from the plants we grow and give them to farmers. Eventually we hope to grow wheat on a large scale that is resistant to drought."

They strolled to the top of a hill and Aaron smiled in pride. He had a wonderful smile and confident, intelligent eyes. "This is our golden harvest," he said.

As she gazed at rows and rows of orange trees covering the slope before her, Henrietta felt a warming in her heart. Here was a man who symbolized the new Jewish state, who was on his own land and free to create a world with his mind and his hands.

That night, as Sophie slept in the room that had been given them in one of the Zikhron Yaacov houses, Henrietta was seized with a tremendous restlessness. She felt as if the land were calling her. She slipped on a coat and went out into the chilly night air.

A path of moonlight cut across the grove and turned the leaves of the orange trees to silver. The great cup of the universe hung above her with its eternal pattern of stars.

She sat on the stone step in front of the house and inhaled deeply. Suddenly it seemed as if she were caught in a great wheel of destiny. The Jewish people were coming back here, taking possession of their birthright. It would be a nation of peace, for this was the mission of the Jew, to teach the way human beings were supposed to be.

But first, and as always, Henrietta's practical, housewifely mind took over . . . there was so much to do, so much work.

She shivered in the night air and drew her coat closer, for it seemed as if a giant hand had pointed at her and said, "YOU!"

"That's absurd," Henrietta argued with this insistent command coming from within herself. "I'm nearly fifty years old. My work is finished."

"You." The word was whispered into her brain, softly, borne on a sudden gust of wind, which brought with it the fragrance of living orange trees.

3

The Challenge Ahead

In 1905, Henrietta Szold had written: "The older I grow, the more do I find myself bound by sexual limitations. I am quite sure if I were a man I would make my point clear—not because my logic would be any clearer, or more convincing, but because by sheer brute force I could make my voice heard."

She was a quiet woman and had a rather small voice. And in 1910 the world did not easily listen to a woman's voice. But when she returned home, Henrietta was so filled with the need to communicate her feelings about Palestine, that she went from meeting to meeting describing what she had seen and exhorting her audiences to support the settlers.

At this point she had access to quite a few groups. First of all, she was the eminent Rabbi Szold's daughter, in itself a recommendation. But she had many achievements, such as the literary work she had done for the Jewish Publication Society, which had brought her respect in her own right. Also, she had made many influential friends in the Zionist movement, foremost of whom was the rabbi of the huge New York congregation, Temple Emanuel, Judah Magnes. So platforms were open to her.

Although the volume of her voice was small, Henrietta had an air of authority and sincerity that kept audiences listening. This did not mean that they agreed with her. Many in her audience had no interest in a Jewish state; in fact, they felt it was a threat to their identity as Americans. "It will only stir people up against us," they said. "If we are concerned with another country, they will think we are not loyal to the United States."

"Why?" argued the Zionists. "Are people whose parents came from Germany, or England, or France accused of having divided loyalties? They are still interested in the land of their ancestors, but they are Americans too."

"This is different," said the anti-Zionists.

The frustrating thing was that many of these people were wealthy Jews who could have provided desperately needed support to the struggling pioneers.

Henrietta continued to speak. She told about the children with trachoma, and the plight of settlers ravaged by disease. She told about Meier Dizengoff and his dream of a new city.

What interested people most were reports about the new kibbutz settlements and other farms. "We can build a state," she declared. "In spite of their hardships, the pioneers work miracles. Where the Arab works two inches deep, the Jew works a foot deep. On an Arab field, the plow can barely move for the stones; on a Jewish field there are no stones."

She told about the newcomers' thirst for knowledge. "Poverty-stricken immigrants from Yemen go into the fields to work and they take their children and they take books. When they have their noon rest, they study and they teach their children."

The women to whom she spoke wanted to know the condition of women in Palestine. Henrietta shrugged. "Women's needs are the last to be considered. Whatever resources are available go to secure farm equipment, and the women cook on primitive stoves. There's a need for someone to speak up for the women, and especially to get them the medical help they need. There is no decent maternity care available."

Although her addresses to public meetings were mainly appeals for funds, when Henrietta met with her little study group, Hadassah, she spoke about her practical ideas.

"If we had more members and more money, we could send nurses to Palestine, especially those trained to work with eye diseases," she told her friends.

Emma Gottheil, the wife of a professor, considered the matter. "Henrietta, if we could raise the money—and it would take a lot more power than our little group possesses—where would we find the qualified nurses? How would we get them to Palestine? Under what authority would they work when they got there?"

Henrietta sighed. Those were hard questions. She had no answers right now, only dreams.

"You know," said Alice Seligsberg, a social worker and Henrietta's closest friend. "I just might go there. There is a need for someone with my training, especially working with children."

Henrietta faced the summer of 1910 with a feeling of disenchantment. It seemed that everything she did was leading to a dead end. She was impatient mostly with her work. Whereas her job with the Jewish Publication Society had once excited her, editing other people's writings didn't satisfy her anymore. She wanted to do something creative on her own.

One person who kept her busy was her nephew Benjamin, son of Bertha and Louis Levin, who came to spend some time in New York to undergo therapy for a speech defect. Henrietta had a special feeling in her heart for the little boy, named after her father. It might have stemmed from the time Benjamin was very little and was staying with Aunt Henrietta and Grandma Sophie. He had a cold and Sophie had put a

Henrietta with her mother and sisters. *From left:* Henrietta, Adele Szold Seltzer, Sophie Szold, Bertha Szold Levin, and Rachel Szold Jastrow.

croup kettle in his room. Somehow, during the night, the little boy overturned the kettle and the scalding liquid had spilled all over him. It was necessary to rush him to the hospital. During the long days of pain, Henrietta sat by his side, reading to him and comforting him. Ever since, there had been a special bond between them.

No matter how involved she was in her work, she took time that summer to go over with Benjamin the exercises the speech therapist had recommended. He learned to slow down and to take deep breaths when he started to stutter. By the end of the summer, his speech had greatly improved.

But when his parents came to take him home, Henrietta

warned them, "It's not only the techniques he's learned to keep from stuttering that are important, but his emotional state as well. He must learn not to get excited and to have the confidence that he can handle whatever comes up."

The mind and heart of a child fascinated Henrietta. Some people thought that if they were given good food and a comfortable environment, children would grow up well. But more and more, she was becoming aware that a child's emotional life required just as much attention as his or her physical nourishment.

Soon after Benjamin had returned to Baltimore, Henrietta received a request that would truly fill her longing to do something creative. The rather disorganized Zionist group asked her to become their secretary, a volunteer position. But Henrietta never rationed her energies in proportion to the amount of money she was paid. Any job she undertook, she did with her whole heart.

When she went to the Zionist office, she was appalled by the chaotic conditions. The workers were completely unsupervised, correspondence and files were neglected, and everyone was blaming everyone else.

Henrietta wrote to Bertha, "Everything I hear makes me realize that I have taken a huge burden on myself and a hopeless task."

Of course, a hopeless task was just what Henrietta needed to get her adrenaline going. She'd had enough of the placid life.

She began with the accounts, which were a complete mess, and often toiled far into the night trying to straighten things out. Her unrelenting conscience wouldn't let her relax. She bewailed in a letter, "I wish, oh I wish I could be confoundedly unconscientious. I hate myself for a prig when people dare to do it to me."

Everyone else was taking off on trips with barely an excuse, but she felt tied to her desk. "If I set a bad example, how can I reprimand others?'' she said to Louis Lipsky, one of the Zionist leaders.

Henrietta's little Hadassah study group continued its modest activities, doing what women's organizations usually did. They read articles and poetry about Zionism to each other and sewed clothing to send to Palestine. But in 1912, thousands of miles away in Basle, Switzerland, a decision was made that was to propel what had been started by a small band of friends into one of the largest women's organizations in the world.

The struggling Zionist movement had managed to gather delegates from many countries to consult with one another at annual conferences, usually held in Switzerland. In 1912, at the tenth Zionist Congress, it was proposed that a women's Zionist organization, to work with the main body, be established. American delegates, who knew about the small ladies' study group and especially about the dynamic Henrietta Szold, proposed that this group be used as the nucleus for an ambitious official women's organization.

The women were tremendously excited. One exclaimed to Henrietta, "Now we can do all the things we dreamed about. Everything is open to us!" to which Henrietta realistically replied, "Yes, it will be done, but it is not so open and easy."

The first meeting of the national Women's Zionist Organization was held in the vestry room of Temple Emanuel in New York City. Forty women were present. Henrietta Szold was elected president. At first, it was decided to call the new organization Daughters of Zion, but affection for their old name, Hadassah, honoring Queen Esther, won out; it was simpler and more distinctive.

At the suggestion of Zionist leader Israel Friedlander, they took as their motto a saying from Jeremiah, "The healing of the daughter of my people." Victor Brenner, the famous sculptor who had designed the Lincoln penny, devised an

The Hadassah seal designed by Victor Brenner

emblem, a Star of David with *Hadassah* in Hebrew super-imposed upon it and the motto above it.

The new organization had $283 in the treasury, but it was nevertheless a national organization. That meant that Hadassah could start branches throughout the country.

It was time to stop fiddling around with petty activities, Henrietta decided. Hadassah would send a nurse to Palestine. But first the organization would have to obtain the funds.

Supported by the clout of representing a national organization, Henrietta went to visit Mr. and Mrs. Nathan Straus, wealthy philanthropists and owners of Macy's department store, who had just returned from a trip to Palestine. Reminding Nathan Straus of the poor blind children stricken with trachoma and the other medical needs so obvious in Palestine, she pleaded with him for funds to send a public health nurse.

Mr. Straus listened gravely. Then he said, "You know, Miss Szold, I have already established a soup kitchen in Palestine. This is because once, long ago, I was starving. I vowed then that no man or woman who crossed my path would go hungry. I also feel that your mission is important. I will give you enough funds to send a nurse to Palestine."

When Henrietta returned to her friends with the miraculous news, they stared at her, flabbergasted. Idle chatter about filling Palestine's medical needs was one thing, but actually taking a bold step like sending a nurse was terrifying. In 1912, women had very little power. They were not even permitted to vote.

"You want us to send a nurse, one woman, into that lion's den!" exclaimed Emma Gottheil. "You know the enormity of the problems in Palestine. What can one woman do?"

"The men will laugh at us if we fail," said another member.

Henrietta looked at the women before her, her dark eyes thoughtful. Every word they said was true. But something impelled her to go ahead. She said, with a firmness she really did not feel, "It is time for our organization to work independently, to go ahead and take risks. If our mission is to be healing, so be it. Now we must get to work."

The women voted to send the nurse.

Curiously, just at that time, another windfall occurred. In Chicago, a woman named Eva Leon persuaded a group of wealthy men to finance the sending of a nurse to Palestine by Hadassah. Now, instead of choosing one nurse, Henrietta needed to find two.

The two nurses who agreed to go were very different from each other, but both extremely capable. Rose Kaplan, the elder of the two, had been a nurse at Mount Sinai Hospital in New York. She was short, stocky, and dark, while the other nurse, Rachel "Ray" Landy, who came from Cleveland, was tall and blonde. Rachel had supervised nurses at Harlem Hospital in New York. Rose signed up for two years, Ray for two and a half.

The nurses went to Palestine accompanied by the Strauses and Eva Leon. With financial aid from Nathan Straus, they furnished a stone house in Mea Shearim, the ultra-Orthodox section of Jerusalem. Over the gate was a sign, AMERICAN DAUGHTERS OF ZION NURSES SETTLEMENT, HADASSAH. On March 23, 1913, they opened their doors. Hadassah's work in Palestine had begun.

The first venture was a maternity hospital. Then the nurses expanded their work to treat victims of trachoma, aided by an eye specialist, Dr. Abraham Ticho, who had come to Palestine.

Meanwhile, the Hadassah organization sponsoring them prospered. It now had two hundred fifty members.

4

Hadassah

Slowly, conditions were beginning to improve in Palestine. More land was reclaimed from the desert and the swamps, and the settlers increased their crops. In Jerusalem, Hadassah's tiny medical organization began to take a stab at mountainous problems.

Then, on July 28, 1914, in Sarajevo, Yugoslavia, an angry Serb assassinated Archduke Francis Ferdinand, heir to the throne of Austria. At that time, two large empires ruled much of Europe and the Middle East. One was the Austro-Hungarian Empire, which had Germany as its ally. The other large empire, whose territories included Palestine, was the Ottoman Empire, ruled by Turkey. These two empires often worked together.

Great Britain and France had always held smoldering hatreds against the Austro-Hungarian Empire and Germany. Following the murder of the Archduke, there were retaliations and counter-retaliations. Somehow, matters became more and more inflamed until all of Europe was at war. France and Great Britain, called the Allies, were fighting their old enemies, the two empires, and Germany. Turkey, the ruler of Palestine, was at war with France and Great Britain.

At that time, Turkey was called the sick man of Europe. Even before World War I, it was plain that the power of the Ottoman Empire was waning. Very often when people feel threatened, they behave irrationally. That was the way the Turks behaved toward the Jewish settlers.

The Turks sensed, correctly, that there was a feeling of friendship between the Jews and England. There had always been British interest in a Jewish state in Palestine. Originally rooted in religious belief, it had changed to something more practical. The British knew that Palestine, in the hands of capable educated Jews, was likely to be an ally in the Middle East, important because of its oil riches.

The Jews, in turn, felt comfortable with the British, whose ideas of government were closer to democracy than those of the Turkish despots. Also, although at that time the United States had not yet entered the war, there was a friendship between the United States and Britain. Many of the needs of Jewish pioneers were supported by money from American Jews.

So, the Turks felt that their subjects, the Palestinian Jews, were their enemies. They instituted cruel measures, which often did not make much sense. The Turkish army took over the lands the Jews had made productive, saying they needed the crops for their armies. They also laid waste many Jewish settlements, including the budding city of Tel Aviv. For the time being, Meier Dizengoff's city was returned to the sand dunes.

The settlers faced terrible deprivation. The loss of their farms brought on a famine. People were dying of starvation and illnesses. Because of the disruption of shipping by the war, it was almost impossible to get help to them.

Aaron Aaronsohn made a special trip to Jerusalem from

his agricultural station to implore the Hadassah nurses to go home while they still could, but they refused. Moreover, another member of Hadassah decided to face the dangers and hardships of wartime Palestine.

Alice Seligsberg, Henrietta's closest friend, came to her and told her that she wanted to use her skills as a social worker where they were needed so desperately. "Children are hungry. Maybe with my social work experience I can help distribute what little food is available in a systematic way."

Henrietta clasped her friend to her. They were so alike, daring to do what everyone said was impossible.

Conditions became more and more critical. For those in America, it was almost impossible to get news of Palestine; the only contact was with a small group in Alexandria, Egypt. Nurse Rose Kaplan, who was not well, managed to get back to the United States for medical treatment, but as soon as she felt better, she attempted to return to Palestine. However, she could get no further than Alexandria, where she died before she was able to reach Jerusalem.

Meanwhile, Ray Landy stayed on, working with the eye specialist. She got word out that conditions were particularly terrible in Jaffa. Finally a doctor, Bertha Kagan, and several Palestinian Hadassah-trained nurses relieved her, and Ray was able to go home.

Henrietta traveled to cities throughout the United States, speaking to the fledgling Hadassah groups and at other meetings, begging for funds to send whatever supplies could trickle into Palestine past the blockades. Several young Palestinians managed to get to the United States and spoke to Zionist and other Jewish groups. There was a thoughtful young man named David Ben-Gurion, with a halo of flyaway hair, and a fiery ex-journalist from Russia named Vladimir Jabotinsky, who had recently changed his first name to Zev.

Jabotinsky was a veteran of the battle of Gallipoli, where he had served with the Palestinian Mule Corps and had also served with the Jewish Legion, aiding the British.

Addressing an early Hadassah meeting

He was hard and strong, with determined features and intense, magnetic eyes. "The Jews must be a warrior people," he declared.

The idea dismayed Henrietta. She thought strife, any kind of battle, whether between individuals or nations, was wasteful tragedy. She declared in 1914, "There are under arms twenty-five million young men and they are being sent out to battle for what purpose? Twenty-five men in the world desire it."

Her bitterness was further deepened by sorrow because Germany was the enemy. German was the native language of her parents, and she spoke it fluently and loved German culture. Hoping that the United States would not be drawn into the war, she joined the People's Council of America for Democracy and Peace.

But peace movements were short-lived. The United States entered the war on the side of the Allies. With a heavy heart, Henrietta felt that as a loyal American she had to support the war effort.

News that brought Henrietta great sorrow came from Palestine. Both Aaron Aaronsohn and his sister Sarah had been engaged in espionage for the British. Sarah was caught and, fearing that if she were tortured she'd betray her friends, she shot herself. Later, Aaron was being flown in a British army plane to London to make a report to the British Secret Service. The plane crashed and he was killed.

Henrietta wept, thinking of Aaron's orange trees, marching like soldiers of peace up the hill.

In 1916, she had another blow. After suffering for months with a lung disease, Sophie Szold died.

Henrietta's work with the Jewish Publication Society had been petering out. The man for whom she worked retired and her own interest was flagging. It seemed that that part of her life was over. More and more of her time was devoted to Zionist causes. But she could not afford to spend all of her time as a volunteer. She had no husband to support her; her inheritance from her parents was not great. She needed a way to earn an income.

This was evident to some prominent Zionists who realized the value of her contribution. Justice Louis D. Brandeis of the U.S. Supreme Court got together several wealthy people who set up a fund that Henrietta could use to support herself as long as she needed it. She managed money very carefully, even funds that were given to her to use for accommodations when she traveled. Later, when she became very famous, she refused to stay at elegant hotels, saving the money of the organization that sponsored her.

During the war years she continued to travel, pleading the

In the headquarters of the World Zionist Organization in New York City. *Seated from left:* Henrietta, Rabbi Stephen Wise, Jacob de Haas, and, *seated fifth from left,* Louis Lipsky.

Zionist cause. But people did not flock to give her money. There were other needs for contributions, and they were very deserving. The war had disrupted conditions in Europe. Many Jews, especially those in Eastern Europe, were in dire need. Some American Jews felt it was more important to send help to their brothers in Europe than to a handful of adventurers in Palestine. The sad thing was that Henrietta had to admit that they had a point.

Other people insisted that there was no need for a Jewish state at all. "People are civilized now. There's little anti-Semitism. Even Russia has a new government that declares anti-Semitism a crime. Let the Jews assimilate in their own countries."

But Henrietta persisted. Somehow, she had an urgent feeling that there must be a Jewish state.

She became so well known that she was asked to speak at Cooper Union, a college in New York City. This was a great honor; the lectures at Cooper Union were famous. Abraham Lincoln had spoken from the very platform where Henrietta stood.

She said of the Jewish people: "Their spiritual and moral characteristics have always remained as enticing ideals in the minds of men." She reminded the audience that the Jewish ideal of moral behavior was exemplified by the way they acquired land in Palestine. "The Jews have not tried to conquer the land and steal it from its inhabitants. They established the Jewish National Fund so all land could be paid for fairly and with the consent of the owner."

The war ended. Turkey, along with Germany, was defeated and the Ottoman Empire was no more. England accepted a mandate from the League of Nations to rule Palestine.

A Jewish chemist, Chaim Weizmann, had contributed a great deal to the British war effort. As a reward, England, through its spokesman, Lord Balfour, issued the Balfour Declaration, which declared that Palestine would eventually become a Jewish state.

Henrietta resumed her work, guiding Hadassah in a renewed effort to provide medical services in Palestine, in conjunction with the American Zionist Medical Unit. But she would be sixty years old in 1920. Her doctor reminded her that her heart had never been strong since a childhood illness. It was time to retire, to read and to express her own talent in writing and to enjoy her growing nieces and nephews.

But first, there was something to take care of. The Zionist organization approached her in despair. Their medical unit in Palestine was in terrible shape, with quarrels, mismanagement, and the monumental problems left by the war. It

Nurses of the first American Zionist Medical Unit as they appeared in 1918, before sailing for Palestine. *First row, from right:* Henrietta, Alice Seligsberg, and, *fourth from right,* Emma Gottheil.

would be necessary for someone to go to Palestine for a little while, just to straighten things out. Inasmuch as Miss Szold, as president of Hadassah, was already involved with the medical services in Palestine, perhaps she could go to Palestine and try to do this?

Henrietta sighed. Retirement would have to wait for a few months. She packed her belongings and set sail for Palestine.

5

Reason, Not Arms

In Jerusalem, Henrietta was given temporary quarters in Dr. Bertha Kagan's house while Dr. Kagan was on vacation. She had three pleasant rooms, including a study, which was her delight. It overlooked a beautiful garden; the profusion of plants that could grow in Palestine's mild climate was a wonder to her. From tree to tree there came a calling of birdsong, of trills and arpeggios and long sweet hoots. As she sat there, entranced, she felt as if she were on an island in space, removed from the quarrels of the American Zionist Medical Unit, the shortages, and Arab riots.

Friday afternoon was her special time to retreat to the garden room and to write to her sisters and friends about her experiences. One of the disappointments of her life was that she'd had no time to use her wonderful talent for writing. That talent showed up in her letters, which her sisters kept and which help us to understand very vividly everything she experienced.

But her peace and quiet were often interrupted. She wrote

to Bertha, "People come in every afternoon and expect to find a cup of tea waiting for them."

The Zionist organization was grateful to her for coming. They did everything possible to make Henrietta comfortable, even furnishing her with a housemaid of her very own. She wrote, in mock despair, "They sent me a Rivka, such a Rivka! But what am I to do? She knows nothing of housework, but she is loyal. And anyhow, the unemployment rate here is horrendous; one cannot possibly discharge an employee."

One Friday afternoon, Henrietta heard a knock at the door, followed by Rivka, her black hair pinned into a knot from which escaping strands streamed. "Ma'am," she said in Yiddish. "There's company. You want I should put up tea?"

"Please," said Henrietta. Sighing, she got up from her letter writing and went into the sitting room.

The visitor turned out to be Dr. I. M. Rubinow, Director of the American Zionist Medical Unit. He sank heavily into a chair. Rivka offered him tea, spilling just a little, and he gulped it gratefully.

He looked bleakly at Henrietta. "They're threatening to strike."

"Who?"

"The medical workers at Tiberias. Miss Szold, I swear I can't take it anymore."

Henrietta hid her panic. Suppose the director quit?

She looked sympathetically at Dr. Rubinow and offered him a piece of cake. "It will be all right," she soothed.

But she wasn't so sure. She had arrived in Palestine to find a hornet's nest of intrigue, complaints, shortages, and plain incompetence. At first she felt overwhelmed, writing to her sister, "It is useless for me to describe the devious politics among the physicians. I fell into the trap the first week after I arrived—that is, I lost my balance. The storm of gossip, rumors, complaints, grievances, charges, malice, and distortions was too much for me. Fortunately, I caught myself before I became completely involved."

Henrietta recognized precisely why she had come to Jerusalem and what her position was. It was not that she was unsympathetic to people's problems, but if she fell into the quicksand with them, then to whom could they appeal? Her job, she thought wryly, was not to sink but to stay on firm ground, a point of stability.

"Our funds are being cut every day and now these people want more money." The director fumed.

"Prices are high," Henrietta remarked.

"Tell that to the Joint Distribution Committee, which is supposed to be sending us funding."

"Well, they must also send funds to Eastern Europe," Henrietta said, trying to sound reasonable. "People there are still suffering from the effects of the war."

Dr. Rubinow put down his cup. The room was silent except for the ticking of a clock.

Apprehension filled Henrietta. She was about to hear something she wasn't going to like. She was right.

"Miss Szold," Dr. Rubinow said finally, "I am planning to return to the United States. Do you think you can manage here while I'm gone? I feel I must report conditions to those who handle the purse strings."

"Of course, of course," she said, forcing herself to sound reassuring. It was all very well to be a rock of calm when someone else was in charge. But now he was turning the whole leaky ship over to her!

"You will return?" she implored.

"Yes, of course," he said.

"Have another sandwich," she offered, praying that he was telling the truth.

At that moment another visitor arrived, Alice Seligsberg, who had worked with social services all during the dangerous days of the war. Her silky black hair, daringly—for 1920—cut short, bounced as she plunked herself down in an easy chair. "I'm exhausted," she said to Henrietta. "Hello, Dr. Rubinow."

"Dr. Rubinow is returning to the United States," said Henrietta.

Alice looked at Henrietta in alarm, already knowing the answer to her question. "Who will take charge?"

"I'll be doing it. Temporarily, I hope." Henrietta looked appealingly at Dr. Rubinow, who remained expressionless.

"Oh dear," said Alice. "This is a bad time to tell you my news. I'm going home."

"But that's splendid, darling. You've earned it. You were a soldier all during the war years caring for children. The other soldiers went home, so should you."

Their eyes met. "Are you sure you won't be lonesome, so far from home?" asked Alice.

"I'll be lonesome but there's a job to do. We'll keep in touch about the trade school idea. If you're in the States you can visit schools and send me ideas."

"With all this medical mess on your hands, you're going to start a trade school?" Dr. Rubinow asked incredulously.

"We weren't planning to do it tomorrow," Henrietta assured him. "But Hadassah's been thinking of it. Sort of an outgrowth of the nurses' school. With economic conditions the way they are in this country, people must be trained in marketable skills. Not everyone can be a farmer."

"I just remembered," said Alice. "Henrietta, I heard from Sophie Berger. She's coming to work for the Red Cross."

"Wonderful," said Henrietta, cheered. The idea of Alice leaving pained her, but Sophie would make a good companion. "Maybe she'll share a house with me."

Other guests from the close-knit American community arrived: Dr. and Mrs. de Sola Pool, Jessie Sampter, the poet, and the Zionist Director of Education, Alex Dushkin. The tea flowed, with Rivka scampering nervously from one to the other, offering cake and sandwiches. Voices rose in agitation. Arab riots had broken out, protesting the Balfour Declaration promising a Jewish state.

"The Arabs have ripped up feather beds and defaced Torahs," declared Alex Dushkin.

"I'm afraid our British friends will not protect us against the Arabs," Dr. de Sola Pool speculated. "Discontented Arabs suit their purpose."

"Why is that?" asked Jessie Sampter.

"You see it's this way," explained the doctor earnestly. "The British want the French out of the Middle East so they can have a monopoly on Arab oil."

"What does that have to do with Arab riots in Palestine?" asked Alice.

"If the Arabs get worked up against the invading Jews in Palestine, their brothers in French-ruled countries might get similar ideas and send the French packing." Dr. de Sola Pool made a tent of his fingers and touched it to his mouth to underline the elegance of his argument. "That would leave the British dominant in the Middle East."

The rest of the company looked at him skeptically. It was all too calculating, but then one never knew about international intrigue.

"On the day of the big riot, the Governor of Jerusalem relieved all Jewish policemen from duty," Alex remarked. "There was no one to oppose the crazy mob."

"Except for Zev Jabotinsky," Jessie muttered, "and do you know what happened to him?"

"I don't know. What happened?" asked Henrietta, recalling the rough-hewn soldier she'd met in the United States.

"Zev Jabotinsky gathered together some of his old buddies from the Jewish Brigade who had fought with British General Allenby during the war. They decided to take matters into their own hands. They had the rioters on the run, but British troops arrived and not only blocked their way, but arrested them. Jabotinsky and his men are imprisoned in an old Crusader fortress near Accra. I hear Zev got fifteen years."

"How horrible," said Henrietta. "I'll be near Accra next week on an inspection tour. I'll go and visit Zev."

At first, Henrietta was dismayed at being propelled into the temporary directorship of the medical units, but then she began to feel exhilarated. She always liked to be in charge of things. When Dr. Rubinow was there, she had considered some ideas for improvements, and she would have liked making suggestions to the director, but she hadn't wanted to undermine his position. Now, with Dr. Rubinow far away in the United States, she could put some of her ideas into effect.

She began by inspecting medical installations, which were scattered throughout the country, mostly in crude makeshift quarters. Hadassah alone had four hundred employees, as she well knew, discontented with working conditions and pay. There were forty-five physicians, often at odds with one another and unable to have good interaction with the nurses. The problem, as one American-trained nurse told Henrietta, was that the doctors and nurses differed in their backgrounds.

American nurses, used to strong leadership from doctors, were dismayed at the haphazard directions they got from physicians from other countries. "They don't know how to issue orders," exclaimed one American Hadassah nurse. Some doctors had ideas about a nurse's role that seemed strange to American nurses; they were annoyed if a nurse dared comment on a patient's condition. German doctors, who had worked with nuns, were amazed that nurses wanted regular working hours.

At the brand-new nurses' school, connected with Rothschild Hospital, there was a shortage of textbooks. "What we need are good nursing textbooks written in Hebrew," one supervisor told Henrietta.

Henrietta was appalled by the poor living conditions of the nurses at Rothschild. "How can these bright young women live in such misery?" she mourned.

Traveling to medical units outside Jerusalem was very dif-

ferent from the journey in 1909 in Israel Shohat's rickety
wagon. Now Henrietta rode grandly in an automobile, with
an armed escort, which she deplored, to protect her from
Arab brigands. But otherwise the situation was the same as
it had been eleven years earlier—chaos. The inefficiency all
around her made her tidy soul churn.

The government had finally brought in some protection
against Arab attacks. Dignified turbaned Sikhs, along with
British soldiers affectionately termed Tommy Atkins, or later,
Tommies, patrolled the roads. But in remote areas, the settlers were taking no chances. Their settlements were surrounded by trenches and protected by sandbags. Earthen
walls were thrown up on the insides of their little wooden
houses.

In spite of the dangers, immigrants were pouring into the
country—impoverished Jews from Eastern Europe and un-
skilled Jews from Arab countries. Malaria, especially, swept
through the newcomers like a scourge. Henrietta visited a
small Zionist hospital in Jaffa, quite a decent institution. It
had a pediatrics ward and surgical facilities, a clinic for eye
troubles, a dental clinic, and a good laboratory. But this small
hospital was far from prepared for the clamoring need; ma-
laria-stricken patients with fevers of 103° were being turned
away.

Facilities in other places made the hospital in Jaffa seem
like a medical marvel. In Tiberias, where the personnel wanted
to strike, the tiny hospital was housed in what had been a
small private home. Henrietta threw up her hands in Safed.
"The kitchen, pantry, and laundry of the clinic should be
condemned," she declared.

As she tried to cope with enormous present difficulties,
Henrietta did not abandon visions of what could be done.
Her aim was not only to establish a fine hospital in Jerusalem,
sponsored by Hadassah, but to provide medical services
throughout the country, devoted to healing and teaching.

She was interested in spreading information about public sanitation, convinced that many of the medical problems in the country were caused by plain filth.

Although her plans seemed like faraway dreams, Henrietta had a feeling that if Hadassah did not retain control of its own work, these dreams would never be realized. She'd seen enough entanglement in red tape by organizations to want to keep away from the larger Zionist organization. This caused a conflict with a man named Ussisskin, head of the local Zionist organization, who felt that Hadassah efforts should be incorporated into the general Zionist medical program.

"No," said Henrietta. "Hadassah will of course cooperate with you and share, but we have to develop in our own way."

As the car rolled to Zikhron Yaacov, where she would pay her respects to the father of Aaron Aaronsohn, a letter to her sisters formulated in Henrietta's mind. She thought of all the difficulties she had to report. Idly she glanced out the window at the rocky soil, reclaimed in places, the stones dug out and irrigation applied and healthy crops replacing the desert. The words came to her, "Hope is not blighted by all of these difficulties, just as the stoniness of the soil doesn't kill one's confidence in the fertility."

This might be so, but there were plenty of stones cluttering up the administration of medical services. The biggest problem was money. About two and a half times the funds they were getting at present were needed, she calculated. However, it was not easy to get the money. She would have to make the resources she already possessed stretch further. Perhaps she could close down all of the other facilities and concentrate on doing a really excellent job in Jerusalem.

Her forehead knotted in worry. That wouldn't do—not with all those settlers pouring into rural areas, living in tents, suffering so many diseases of deprivation. No, she needed more facilities, not fewer.

Resolutely, she cleared her mind for the meeting with Mr. Aaronsohn.

Her heart was heavy when she saw what was left of Aaron's proud agricultural station. Everything had fallen into disrepair and the gardens were given over to weeds. Aaron's brother had managed to gather some of the papers and collections, but many objects were broken and strewn around or decayed into dust.

Mr. Aaronsohn, mourning for his son Aaron and his daughter, Sarah, told Henrietta that the station was hounded by creditors. "They think I got a settlement of money for the death of my son," he wept. "But I got nothing."

Sadly, Henrietta left the ruined farm and went back to the coast. Before turning off on the road to Jerusalem, she stopped at Accra, visiting the ancient Crusader fortress where Zev Jabotinsky and his followers were imprisoned. The blackened stone walls towered ominously, grim witnesses to wave upon wave of men bent on destroying one another. Slits in the towers had been the openings for Crusader arrows. Cannonballs fired by Napoleon's artillery were still embedded in the walls.

Yet in a bleak courtyard Henrietta came upon one of Jabotinsky's men drying specimens of plants. "I'm a botanist," he explained. "Some amazing specimens grow right here, inside the walls." Warming to her interest, he listed the odd Latin names of his plants. "Just think," he said with a wry smile. "If I hadn't been arrested, I would not have had this opportunity."

Henrietta grinned; she couldn't help it. "You'll be freed soon," she assured him.

"Maybe." He shrugged, and went on with his work.

Zev Jabotinsky, full of defiant vigor, paced his cell. Henrietta gave him a bundle of food and other comforts. He put them on a grimy shelf and sat down next to her on a rickety bench.

"I'm grieved for you. Zev. Fifteen years out of your life! You are—"

"Forty," he said. "If I were to stay here fifteen years, I'd be fifty-five. But you mustn't believe it, Miss Szold. That sentence was for the benefit of public opinion, Arab public opinion," he jeered. "The British have to play their little games, to keep the Arabs happy. I'll be released soon."

"I hope so," she said.

She liked Zev, found him fascinating. But she did not like the hatred that gleamed from his eyes.

"No one will hand us our freedom," he declared. "We must fight all who stand in our way. We must fight the Arabs and fight the British."

She regarded him with her soft brown eyes, in their own way just as compelling as his fiery ones. "The purpose of a Zionist state is not to put one more warring nation on earth. We need to make friends with our neighbors and understand them, to resolve conflicts through reason, not through arms," she said.

He stood up and faced her, his hands on his hips. "First," he said, "we must secure the land."

She could not disagree with that. She wished him well and left for Jerusalem.

A short time later, as he had predicted, Zev Jabotinsky was released from prison.

6

"The Healing of the Daughter of My People"

The British were not unmindful of Jewish public relations in their administration of the Mandate. When the new post of High Commissioner was established in June 1920, the man appointed to fill the position was a British Jew, Sir Herbert Samuel.

Sir Herbert and his family arrived amid great pomp, especially aimed at impressing the Arab population, which had a feeling for glittering chiefs. All the way from Jaffa up to Jerusalem, turbaned Sikhs and immaculate Tommies stood with rifles at the ready as the motorcade passed. This was not completely ceremonial. Considering the unstable conditions in the country, the rifles were loaded.

Shortly after the splendid arrival of the High Commissioner, an even more spectacular event occurred. Sir Herbert and Lady Samuel's son was married. Henrietta, who was acquainted with the bride, was invited to the wedding.

The wedding was magnificent. It required three rabbis under

an ornate canopy to unite the couple. Arab sheikhs and tribal chieftains turned up in royal glory and vied to outdo one another in the extravagance of their gifts. The gift that seemed to top everything was a small remembrance from a Druse chieftain: an entire village with all its inhabitants!

"After the wedding," Henrietta wrote to her sisters, "I traveled down the hill and went into my office and worried about money."

Henrietta estimated that her deficit was about 1,200 British pounds a month (around $3,000) and growing every day as needs increased. Each day she had to make excruciating decisions, allotting her sparse funds. Should a doctor be kept at a pioneer settlement, where most of the inhabitants were young and healthy but wounds from an Arab attack might need prompt care? Or should the doctor be placed in a city clinic?

Quarrels and demands of the staff continued, but Henrietta maintained her point of stability and kept from taking sides. Her sense of humor, especially her view that people who argue are ridiculous, lightened the atmosphere.

"I had an argument with our dermatologist today," she told her housemate, Sophie Berger. "He's our thin-skinned specialist. Come to think of it, he's no specialist. They're all thin-skinned."

Sophie Berger filled Alice Seligsberg's place in Henrietta's life in Palestine. The two women rented a little stone house, which, to Henrietta's delight had a wonderful garden with prolific flowers of many kinds and trees bearing olives, plums, figs, and oranges. The whole place was covered with a riot of flowering vines. The little house became a haven for their friends, especially those from the American community. They gave dinner parties for which Sophie did most of the cooking; Henrietta was much too busy.

Her job continued its relentless demands. Henrietta sometimes called herself a beast of burden. Often she wondered what a woman nearly sixty years old was doing trotting all over the country and unraveling problems that would have confounded a sage.

It was painful to recognize people's needs and not be able to fill them. "Today I had forty people come to my office, asking for jobs," she told her friends. "They wouldn't believe me when I told them that although we certainly could use more help, we had no money to pay them. They think Americans are bottomless pits of money."

Henrietta was determined to be firm, to refuse to see any more begging people, but her soft heart always prevailed. One day an old couple, who had traveled all the way from Haifa to Jerusalem, showed up.

"We are trying to make a living from a machine that makes stockings and some hens that lay six eggs a day," they explained. "All we need is a loan of fifteen pounds to pay our debts."

Sighing, Henrietta dug into a fund established by Rabbi Stephen Wise of New York for miscellaneous charities.

One day a tall Arab appeared. Henrietta greeted him politely. After the unrest of the previous year, she was anxious to establish good relationships between Arabs and Jews.

Regally, the man walked up to Henrietta's desk and kissed her hand. Speaking through an interpreter, he informed her that he was the Sheikh of the Mosque of Omar.

"What can I do for you?" Henrietta asked.

The sheikh pulled himself up proudly. "I have five daughters. My family is starving. I need some money."

Henrietta looked at him skeptically. "Come back in a few days and we'll see what we can do." Certain that the man was a fake, she was going to investigate him.

"I will not return," he said. "I have come to ask for help once. If you give it to me, I will take it. But I will not ask again."

Shamed by the man's pride, Henrietta reached into her sparse funds and took out a pound for him.

He stopped and, with utmost dignity, kissed the hem of her dress.

"Who told you to come to see me?" she asked.

He crossed his hands across his stomach and gave her a piercing glance. "A-l-l-a-h," he said with great deliberation.

Henrietta bowed her head. "There is but one favor I would like to ask you in exchange for my help. I would like to see the inside of the Mosque of Omar. I have often admired it."

With a flourish, the man took out a card and wrote his name on it. Giving it to Henrietta, he said, "You will come on Sunday." Then he went to the door, turned, and raised his hand to his lips and forehead, and left.

The next Sunday, Henrietta was one of the first non-Moslems to enter the Mosque of Omar.

After a reverent few moments in this house of worship, she left with a dream in her heart. She visualized a Semitic Confederation of Palestine, in which Arabs and Jews would mold a modern nation, bringing prosperity and security to both.

Demands for her time and energy continued to beat down upon Henrietta, as she put it, "with the same intensity as the rays of the sun" during the hot summer months. Like an oasis in the midst of weariness, discouragement, and homesickness was the Hadassah nursing program.

Henrietta felt as though the young nurses and student nurses were her daughters. In a symbolic way, they were her daughters, bringing to life the Hadassah motto, The Healing of the Daughter of My People. She was concerned with their personal happiness, their comfort, and the quality of their training. One of the first things she did was to find textbooks written in Hebrew, a common language all of these people from many countries shared. Since modern Hebrew was so new, many adaptations had to be made. Modern medical terms had to be translated into the ancient language; in many cases the easiest solution was simply to adopt English words into Hebrew.

Planting a tree with nurses in 1920

The nurses ignored the fact that Henrietta was older than some of their mothers; they accepted her as one of themselves. One summer evening Henrietta, along with the nurses and their boyfriends, went for a picnic on top of Mount Scopus near Jerusalem. They were a noisy crowd, singing Hebrew songs and dancing horahs. Although she always sang off-key, Henrietta loved singing and dancing.

Finally, they all sat on the grass and looked contentedly down the mountain toward Jerusalem, the "city of gold," its buildings of golden stone gilded and rosy in the sunset. On the other side of the mountain they could see in the distance the silver mirror of the Dead Sea in the middle of the sable-colored desert.

"On this spot," declared Henrietta, "we shall build a great hospital."

One of Henrietta's favorite nurses was a young woman named Shulamit Yedid-Halevey. Shulamit was the daughter of prosperous Jews in Beirut, Lebanon. To her parents' dismay, she had insisted upon studying nursing at the American Hospital in Beirut; in those days, wealthy Jewish girls just didn't do that sort of thing.

Shulamit had a dream, to nurse in Palestine. In September of 1918, a boatload of men, war refugees, was leaving Beirut for Palestine. Shulamit persuaded her cousin, one of the passengers, to hide her behind some beds.

The ship sailed under starry skies. The evening was balmy. Someone began playing a lively horah on an accordion and soon the deck was thumping with the boots of men dancing.

Shulamit could not restrain herself. She ran out from her hiding place and joined the circle of dancers. Naturally, as the only woman dancing, she was quickly spotted. The angry captain decided to turn the ship around and take Shulamit back to Beirut.

"Oh please," begged Shulamit. "I'm a registered nurse. I only want to serve in Palestine."

A woman who had been standing nearby approached the captain. He looked at her respectfully; she was Mrs. Ticho, wife of the famous eye doctor, who was returning with her husband to Palestine from a trip.

"I couldn't help but overhear," she said. "Captain, I implore you, please allow this young lady to come to Palestine. My husband is connected with the Hadassah health services, and their need for trained nurses is enormous."

Reluctantly, the captain allowed Shulamit to proceed to Palestine, where she was turned over to the American Zionist Medical Unit. Eventually, the young stowaway became Supervisor of Nurses at Hadassah Hospital and then Director of the Nursing School, where she served for many years.

In the fall, somewhat to Henrietta's surprise, Dr. Rubinow returned as he had promised. A little regretfully, Henrietta gave up her temporary administrative job. In spite of all the

Dr. I. M. Rubinow, Henrietta's predecessor as Director of the American Zionist Medical Unit, stands with Henrietta in Jerusalem.

difficulties, she felt like a craftsman who has done a good job. "I have never done a bigger piece of work and I have derived some satisfaction from the fact that in spite of my three-score years, I had elasticity enough to turn to a new field of problems and solve them," she said.

She was free to return to the United States, but she had started a number of projects in Palestine. She didn't feel she could leave until they were well under way. Now that she had more time, no longer tied to the director's job, she was able to travel around the country checking like an anxious mother on the condition of all the medical installations she had started and the well-being of the settlers, young men and women who were close to her heart.

7

Hour of Trial

In November the rains came, cleansing chalky dust from plants and revitalizing the dry earth. Orange blossoms appeared on the trees and the gnarled olive trees in the backyard yielded a harvest, which Henrietta and Sophie triumphantly served to their guests.

But the rains also brought mud and chill. The short flapper skirts of the twenties were not to come into fashion for several years, and women still wore long dresses reaching to the tops of their shoes. Impatiently, tired of rims of mud on her skirts, Henrietta had her dresses cut short, anticipating the whims of Paris. Alice Seligsberg had left her a pair of riding boots that she wore when visiting soggy farming outposts, but more than anything, she longed for a good pair of high rubber boots.

The little stone house, built to keep cool in hot weather, was damp and chilly. As she worked, Henrietta sat, teeth chattering, bundled in sweaters and shawls. Sometimes she had to go outdoors to warm up.

Dressed to explore the countryside of Palestine

As she sloshed from one settlement to the other, she found dismaying conditions. The pioneers were living eight to a rain-soaked tent, plagued by vermin and suffering from malaria, dysentery, and typhoid. The British mandatory government did little for them.

"The immigration medical work was thrust upon Hadassah," Henrietta declared impatiently in a letter, "but those who flung it at us forgot to throw the appropriation of funds with it."

Gradually, out of needs, some beginnings of solutions emerged. There was not only a shortage of food, but many of the pioneers lacked the knowledge of proper nutrition. Henrietta asked an American nutritionist, Yehudit Aronson, to go to a settlement of workmen at a place called Migdal. Yehudit found the workers living on herring, badly baked bread, and tough bully beef from Australia. Deciding to give them something really nutritious, she scurried around and found some old-fashioned oatmeal, which she had the cooks prepare for their breakfast.

The men were furious. "Give us back our herring!" they cried.

Finally, after making friends with them, Yehudit was able to persuade them to change their eating habits just a bit, to include healthier food.

Sanitary conditions were horrible. In some places, people were drinking unpurified water that came from the same rivers in which they dumped their sewage.

When Henrietta protested, one of the settlers laughed. "In America you are soft; everything has to be scrubbed and sanitary. Miss Szold, you're in pioneering territory here. We're tough, used to hardships."

"But is this necessary?" she asked.

Later, when typhoid broke out, the settlers changed their minds. Dysentery was bad enough, but typhoid was going too far. They consented to have inoculations, to cover their toilets, and to boil water. In the early 1920s, 144 out of every 1,000 Jewish children in Palestine died before their first birthday. Statistics regarding Arab children were not available, but were probably worse.

Hadassah instituted a campaign to improve the health of children in the schools. Henrietta's old friend Nathan Straus financed school lunches to make sure the children got at least one good meal a day.

Hadassah also created milk stations, called Tipat Halav, or Drop of Milk, offering pasteurized milk to small children. When mothers were unable to get to the milk stations, the milk was sent to them on the backs of donkeys, a system that became known as the Donkey Express. The donkeys carried bottles packed with ice and labeled with the names of individual babies right to their homes.

Not only did the schoolchildren have free lunches, but Hadassah nurses weighed them and tested them for tuberculosis, as well as for eye and ear diseases. Treating illnesses before they became serious and providing better nutrition worked a change in Palestine's youngsters. Formerly pale, listless children now ran around with robust energy.

Trachoma, the blinding disease that had horrified Henrietta and her mother in 1909, was still common. Hadassah doctors and nurses waged an all-out war against the disease. Ophthalmologists like Dr. Ticho and a young doctor, Haim Yassky, who later became the Director of Hadassah Hospital, tested and treated children in the schools. The doctors also made donkey-back trips to remote settlements and visited children in their homes.

By 1930, the disease was practically wiped out among Jewish children, but as late as 1938, 64 out of every 100 Arab children still suffered from it. Henrietta's dream was to wipe out barriers of communication with the Arabs so their children would attend the schools and be available for treatment.

When Hadassah hospitals were finally established on Mount

Scopus and, later, at Ein Karem, their goal was to provide good health not only for Jews but for Arab citizens as well. Fortunately, some Arab leaders were educated enough to see the value of excellent Hadassah medical care and took advantage of the facilities. This led the way for other Arabs to have the courage to use Hadassah medical services.

Henrietta realized that good health requires not only medicine and proper food, but exercise in the open air. Children in the farming settlements had no problem with that, but in the cities they didn't get out to play very often. Through a gift made by Bertha Guggenheimer of Virginia, a large playground was established just inside the walled city of Jerusalem. It was on the edge of the Jewish quarter, as well as adjoining the Arab area, and was used by Arab and Jewish children.

When it was reported that there were to be showers at the playgrounds, Arab parents were aghast. "Naked boys and girls standing together in the street, showering. It's indecent!"

It was necessary to take the Arab parents for a tour of the playground and to show them that the showers were inside the building and were separate for boys and girls. They'd never heard of inside showers.

Other objections came from Orthodox Jews. "Frivolous. Children should spend their time studying, not running around on a playground."

Rachel Swarz, the future mother-in-law of Moshe Dayan, the famous general, was in charge of the playground. She went to the chief rabbi, Abraham Isaac Halevy Kook, and demanded, "How can you stop children from playing? Can't you see that if they exercise they will be healthier and better able to study?"

The rabbi looked at her thoughtfully. Then he nodded and said, "My daughter, go back to your work and all will be well."

Although Hadassah was growing, with chapters through-out the United States and a membership of ten thousand hardworking women, there was still a shortage of funds for all of these projects. Henrietta journeyed to Paris and sought out Baron de Rothschild, who had invested large sums in Palestine and founded a hospital. But this time he was un-willing to help. "Go to America for money," he told her. Sadly, she left his luxurious office decorated with precious oil paintings, thinking bitterly that one of those paintings was worth enough to feed several children for a year.

But for Henrietta, all had not been hard work and a struggle for funds. There were celebrations too.

Her sixtieth birthday, December 21, 1920, turned out to be a rare sunny day during the rainy season. Sophie said, "Let's celebrate with a picnic."

Henrietta couldn't think of a better way to mark her birth-day. They went up to the hills near Ramallah and picnicked on the rocks. Feeling like a child in a toy shop, Henrietta wandered the hills, picking a treasure of flowers—flaming red or lilac anemones, mandrakes, dwarf white iris, and as-phodel.

As they drove back to Jerusalem, Sophie said, "A picnic is not enough for a birthday. How about our showering and putting on our nicest dresses and going to a hotel for dinner? My treat."

Henrietta was about to protest that she'd already had enough of a good time, but there was a mysterious expression in Sophie's eyes that impelled her to say "All right."

Although she suspected a plot, Henrietta was not prepared for the reception that greeted her when she got to the hotel. Friends had come from all over Palestine. Even Sir Herbert and Lady Samuel had been invited.

Gifts and messages poured in from all over the world, but there were two gifts that Henrietta treasured above all others. After the dinner, a pretty dark-haired young woman approached. "Miss Szold, I don't know whether you remember me. I'm Rifka Aaronsohn, Aaron's sister."

Lovingly, Henrietta held both of Rifka's hands. "Of course I remember you, the little girl who was always butting in, trying to find out what her brothers and sister were up to. How beautifully you have grown up. Your father must be proud of you."

Rifka hung her head. "Papa is still sorrowful. All the shattered dreams. But I try to bring some happiness into his life." Then she smiled, that brilliant, bursting Aaronsohn grin. "I brought you some gifts."

"You shouldn't have," Henrietta began to protest. She knew the Aaronsohns had little to spare for presents. But the words dried on her lips when Rifka handed her a botany book, inscribed on the flyleaf with Aaron's name.

"He knew how you loved flowers," said Rifka. "He'd want you to have this. Now here is something else, very special. Actually, Aaron had this made for you, to give to you in appreciation of the help you gave to him during the visit he made to the United States before the war."

Henrietta removed the wrapping from a large package and found a beautiful jar of Damascus ware. It was filled with grapefruits and tangerines.

"The fruit is from Papa and me," said Rifka softly.

A year later there was another very exciting celebration. On December 7, 1921, the first class of the Hadassah Nursing School graduated. In their crisp white uniforms with the blue Star of David emblazoned on their caps, the new nurses, led by Anna Kaplan, marched into the auditorium of the recently constructed nurses' home, Bet Aminoff. Henrietta presided at the graduation and Lady Samuel handed out the diplomas.

Henrietta said to the nurses, "For this day you have waited three years and, across the world in the United States, Hadassah women have been waiting for eight years. When they sent two pioneer nurses here to inaugurate District Visiting Nursing, they thought of this evening."

The first graduating class of the Hadassah Nursing School

The Hadassah nurses had reason to be proud. Working twelve-hour days, they'd developed professional skills that enabled them to do many things on their own that nurses had not done before. To be a Hadassah nurse in Palestine became a mark of distinction. It is so to this day, when Hadassah nursing standards are recognized throughout the world as an example for others.

8

An Uneasy Peace

Henrietta stayed in Palestine until May 1923, endlessly journeying from one part of the country to the other, checking up on Zionist and Hadassah projects, planning new ones, and making difficult decisions for the allocation of ever-meager funds.

When she returned to the United States, she went directly to a seaside resort, Far Rockaway, near New York City, where her sister Rachel was spending the summer in the hopes that the sea air would restore her frail health. Rachel had been ill off and on for several years with a number of ailments. She did not seem to be able to shake off ill health. Later, she developed a brain tumor.

As happened to Henrietta so often in her life, she was torn between responsibilities. She longed just to stay by Rachel's side, caring for her. But when the members of Hadassah, both locally in Far Rockaway and across the country, learned that she had returned to the United States, they clamored to see her. Henrietta couldn't refuse. There was so much to tell, to let the American people know about Palestine's needs.

"Infant welfare, prenatal care and education, mothers' classes in nutrition and sanitation, anti-tuberculosis work, draining the swamps to get rid of malaria." She detailed the projects that were vital to Palestine. "We need to have instruction, and textbooks in a galaxy of languages: Hebrew, Arabic, Yiddish, Spagniol [spoken by Sephardic, non-European, Jews]," she added.

Although donations for Hadassah medical projects were increasing, fund-raising was an uphill road. In 1923, the needs of Palestine seemed quite remote to Americans. Women enjoyed getting together in a sociable way, but they had not yet learned how to persuade people to make contributions or how to run successful fund-raising campaigns. These skills were developed later, but during the twenties, organizations did not yet have professional fund-raisers and they made many mistakes. Henrietta Szold was clever at devising ways to run a successful organization. At this time, Hadassah women were still learning from Henrietta and depended on her a good deal.

After every meeting she hurried back to Rachel's side.

Her doctors told her to relax. "After all, you're sixty-two. You have to slow down."

Henrietta promised to do so when she had time.

Back in Palestine, matters were starting to unravel. Dr. Rubinow left for good and it was necessary to break in a new director. The Zionist organization asked Henrietta to return for six months.

"I can't," she said desperately. "My sister is very ill. She needs me. Not to mention Hadassah, which depends upon me for decisions."

She was finally persuaded to go for three months.

During the next few years, Henrietta constantly shuttled back and forth between Palestine and the United States. Travel by airplane was not yet common, and her journeys were long

With friends in Riverdale, New York, 1923

trips by ship. Although those were peaceful years in Palestine, for Henrietta they were filled with anxiety. During her time in the United States, she fretted about her projects in Palestine. When she returned to Palestine, she worried about her family, particularly about Rachel, who remained in poor health.

Another grief was the death of Bertha's husband, Louis Levin. Not only did she sorrow for her sister's grief, but the loss of Louis was a keen one for herself. Their relationship, based on similar literary work, had been close.

Teenager Benjamin Levin also worried her. He was an unsettled boy, never seeming to finish anything he started.

"Would you like to come to Palestine someday?" she asked him.

His eyes lit up. "To be a pioneer? That sounds like fun."

"It isn't fun. It's a very hard life. There are no red carpets spread out, but perhaps you would like it."

Leaving for Palestine once again in March 1926, Henrietta was full of foreboding about Rachel. During the trip she wrote to Bertha, "Can you imagine how I find the courage to put 7,000 miles between us? I wonder and wonder until I am reduced to a mere automaton in all that relates to life outside the wondering."

She debarked at Jaffa and got into the small boat that would carry her to the city. A huge wave came along and tilted the boat, sending her to her knees. Henrietta righted herself and crawled to a seat, tears flooding her eyes. It wasn't the pain in her knees that troubled her; it was the pain in her heart, the feeling that she was losing her beautiful sister.

But then, as she rode through the lusciously green countryside, abloom with flowers, her love for the land was rekindled.

The medical services had a new director, Dr. E. M. Bluestone. Henrietta was thankful that she had come to guide him through the shoals of quarrels and shortages that had become so familiar to her.

Not only were there quarrels and jealousies within the medical organizations, but now Hadassah was beginning to be attacked by the very people they were in Palestine to help. A labor organization called the Keren Ha-Yesod, the forerunner of what later became Israel's powerful Labor Party, resented the power of the American organization. Henrietta found herself constantly fencing with them, insisting upon the independence of Hadassah projects when others wanted to swallow them up in different organizations.

Hadassah forged on with new projects, in spite of these attacks. As contributions from America increased, money was available to build small hospitals in Haifa and Tel Aviv. Henrietta went shopping for land. She wrote of her exacting specifications to Rachel: "I'm looking for a piece of land so located that mothers and children can easily reach it. Land that is not in litigation and does not belong to forty heirs, of whom most are minors, or does not belong to forty separate owners, one owner to each square foot, the landmarks between the portions having been removed generations ago and the registry having been lost. Hopefully, it will be large enough for our purposes and not cost as much as the block on Fifth Avenue from 42nd to 43rd in New York City."

This fooling letter was intended to bring a smile to Rachel's face, but buying land was certainly complicated in Palestine, where ownership had meandered through families for hundreds of years. The Jewish National Fund, using funds collected from small sums contributed by poor Jews all over the world, was engaged in disentangling legal titles and buying the land.

The Zionists were determined not to steal anything. At a Zionist Congress in Vienna in 1925, Chaim Weizmann declared, "Palestine must be built up without violating the legitimate interests of the Arabs . . . not a hair of their heads shall be touched."

Henrietta joined a group organized by land developer and head of the Jewish Agency, Arthur Ruppin, called Brith Shalom (Peace Covenant) whose purpose was promoting better understanding among Arabs and Jews. Henrietta's old friend, Rabbi Judah Magnes, who had come to Palestine to become Chancellor of the new Hebrew University on Mount Scopus, was also a member.

In order to show that he did not favor the Jews and was sympathetic also to Arab feelings, High Commissioner Samuel appointed a popular Arab leader, Haj Amin Husseini, as Mufti of Jerusalem, a religious post with tremendous power and prestige among Moslems. This was a terrible mistake. Husseini wanted only one thing, control of Palestine. He was willing to lie and plot to get it. In later years, he became a close friend of Adolf Hitler's. It was only natural; they both wanted the same thing, the annihilation of the Jews. But in the 1920s, the Mufti's plots were mere mutterings of false-hoods. At that time, Zionism was a weak movement, not popular among world Jewry. The Mufti felt that the idea of a Jewish state would soon wither away of its own accord, and so had not yet unleashed the full power of his malev-olence.

Just how feeble the Zionist movement was is expressed in a letter Henrietta wrote to her admiring friend Manya Shohat on October 3, 1927, after returning from a Zionist Congress in Switzerland and a follow-up meeting in London.

"Yes, my intentions are good, free from self-interest—so much I can say. But what of my knowledge, my experience with affairs, my strength, my wisdom? What indeed can the wisest and strongest among us do when we are faced by deficits, a curtailed budget, a problem of eight thousand un-employed? What can a movement do, which in its hour of trial has to resort to a woman of sixty-seven, a tired woman who wanted rest and needed rest?—a movement which ap-parently has developed no personnel—no men, no sacrificial spirits.

"I wish I could feel about myself as you feel about me. I confess to you that I have not had a moment of serenity since the Congress. I have just come from the organizing meeting of the new Executive in London. The whole panorama of problems was unrolled before us—the inadequacy of our prospective means was made cruelly clear. And I have acute personal difficulties—certain duties towards my family, and, worst of all, a commitment to outsiders [the American Ha-dassah organization] to which I am pledged, and which I can meet only in New York.

"I must return to the question of confidence in me. The election did not show that others share it. The Right voted against the combination [a group including Henrietta], and the Left abstained from voting. . . .

"When I went to America last April the situation I found in our American organization was as deplorable as the situation I had seen in Palestine. We had to plunge into the sea of our troubles and difficulties—a deficit of $136,000, no money coming in for the United Palestine Appeal, opposition to the existing management without having others to put in their place.

"All we can do is to make ourselves whole and sound. In America at least that is the only method of restoring confidence. In certain cases all a physician can do is to treat each symptom of a disease as it appears. That must be our method now."

Henrietta felt that if the Zionists would stop quarreling among themselves and get something constructive done, it would make a favorable impression on those who were to donate to the cause. But she was mightily discouraged at that point.

Her depression was further deepened when she received the telegram she had dreaded: RACHEL DYING. COME HOME AT ONCE.

Henrietta caught the next boat to the United States. A few weeks after she arrived home, the brain tumor that had been torturing Rachel finally claimed its victim. Grieving, recalling the young girl who had brightened their childhood home with her singing and dancing, Henrietta still remembered that life had to go on. No matter how discouraging her work seemed, she couldn't quit.

Sadly, she returned to Palestine.

The British mandatory government was anxious to maintain the goodwill of the Arabs, who controlled Middle East oil. They created a committee, headed by Winston Churchill, who later became the wartime British Prime Minister, to study conditions in Palestine.

The committee published a document called a White Paper, giving lands east of the Jordan River to the Arabs and creating a new nation, Transjordan, now called Jordan. An Arab chief, Abdullah, was made king of Jordan.

The Jews weren't too happy about the White Paper, which

reduced their territory. The Arabs weren't pleased either because the agreement chopped up their land into small countries. They would have preferred one large nation, Syria.

At least, however, there was an uneasy peace between Arabs and Jews.

Then on August 23, 1929, the peace in Palestine was shattered. Suddenly Arab rioters attacked hospitals at Mekor Haim, Talpiot, and Moza.

"The babies! They must be brought to safety," Henrietta ordered.

Hastily, the infants in the hospitals were transferred to safer places.

The rioting, which lasted for eight days, spread throughout the country from Safed to Hebron. The Arabs killed 133 Jews and wounded 330.

When the riot had simmered down, the reason for the outburst was uncovered. Someone, probably the Mufti, had spread the ridiculous lie that the Jews were going to tear down the Mosque of Omar and build a synagogue on the site.

Although the riot was of short duration, it reminded the Jews of danger seething below the surface. Zev Jabotinsky's words, "We must protect ourselves," rang through the Jewish settlements. Under the rules of the Mandate, the Jews were not permitted a fighting force, although Israel Shohat's Shomrim had been protecting settlements.

Secretly, a fighting group called Haganah assembled and trained fighters. Weapons were smuggled into the country and kept in hiding in case they were needed. In later years, the soldiers of the Haganah, renamed the Israel Defense Forces, saved the country during the War of Liberation.

Palestine was in the hands of the young and strong and, at last, Henrietta was going home. She wrote, "I leave promptly on September 30, 1929 . . . if I last so long. Don't infer that I am physically not fit. I am as strong as a horse. It's my soul that will perish."

She would be sixty-nine in December. It was time to take her ease.

In Germany, a crazy housepainter with a funny mustache was leading mobs shouting obscenities at the Jews. As Henrietta sailed home, little did she realize that the insane Hitler was devising a new career for her that would eclipse anything she had ever done.

9

Youth Aliyah

Henrietta had barely settled into the luxury of retirement when she received astounding news. A government had been established in Palestine with a legislature called the Knesset. The Labor Party, the same group that had bedeviled her with their sabotage of Hadassah projects, had elected her to the Va'ad Leumi, the National Council of the General Assembly of the Knesset.

"They can have their government without you," her sister Bertha stormed. "You've given enough to Palestine. Now you belong with us."

"It's just for a little while, until things get going," Henrietta promised.

Reluctantly, she set sail for Palestine once again.

Back in Jerusalem, besides her work in the Knesset, Henrietta devoted herself to establishing an orderly system of social services, particularly family agencies and child care. Meanwhile, the country was still embroiled in squabbles, with different groups convinced that only they knew the truth.

There were the Socialists, with whom Henrietta personally sympathized, who hoped to have an Arab-Jewish state. And there were the Conservatives, especially those who were orthodox in religion, who seemed to want to put boxes of do's and don'ts around everything people did. The most troublesome group was the Revisionists, led by fiery Zev Jabotinsky. They would settle for nothing less than a Jewish state, extending beyond the Jordan and incorporating Transjordan.

The Revisionists were not content with oratory; sometimes they resorted to terrorist acts. This alarmed the British, who, in order to placate the Arabs, restricted Jewish immigration.

In October 1934, Henrietta saw the realization of a dream, a ceremony marking the beginning of construction of the great Hadassah Hospital alongside Hebrew University, on Mount Scopus. After an introduction by Judah Magnes, she laid the cornerstone of the building.

Before her, a throng of people, many of whom had worked with her to reach this day, waited in hushed silence for her words. The shining gold buildings of Jerusalem climbed the hills, peaceful in the bright sunshine. In the distance rose Mount Nebo, from which Moses had sighted the Promised Land.

When Henrietta spoke, she told of the beginnings of Hadassah and recited the words of the prophet Jeremiah, the watchwords of the organization, "The healing of the daughter of my people." Then she continued: "The Jewish soul stands in need of the healing which wells up for it from the soil that produced the prophets. In the life of the spirit, there is no ending that is not a beginning."

And she thought not only of the Jewish soul, for to Henrietta one human being was never separate from another, but a part of all those billions throughout the world who

Groundbreaking for the Hadassah Hospital on Mount Scopus, 1934. David Ben-Gurion stands at far left. *Inset:* Henrietta, nine years earlier, at the Hebrew University cornerstone ceremony. Judah Magnes (holding shovel) is at left.

longed for a cleansing so their shining selves could be seen.

The cornerstone laying of Hadassah Hospital was a joyous occasion during a time when there were few joys. In Germany, the housepainter had not been idle. The Nazis had deposed the old German president and Adolf Hitler had come into power. In 1933, the German government had published an Aryan Decree, which spelled out discrimination against the Jews.

Many Jews in Germany lulled themselves into believing that this was but a temporary situation. The crazy brown-shirted Nazis would disappear and all would be as it had been for over a thousand years. These Jews were German to their very bones, had fought in Germany's wars, and had contributed to German culture. Their children's future was in Germany.

But Recha Freier, a slim German woman with intense dark eyes, a rabbi's wife and writer of children's stories, was frightened. She had the feeling that the future for Jewish children in Germany would be dismal. "We must send the youngsters to Palestine," she declared. "There they will have a future."

German parents threw their arms about their children. "Send our precious children to a strange country with no comfort? Never!"

A trickle of German Jews, mostly educated people who had lost their jobs because of anti-Jewish edicts, began to come to Palestine. Although once well off, many of them had used up their money and they depended on Palestine social services for help.

Support from Jews in other countries had always kept the people of Palestine going. Now it was the Palestinians' turn to help. Henrietta journeyed to a prosperous orange grove in Petah Tikvah and sat beneath a palm tree, inhaling the fragrance of growing jasmine. Around her were seated the members of a committee that had been sent to meet with her and discuss German relief.

"The Germans never liked us," scoffed the Russian-descended settlers. "They always thought they were superior. Why should we help them? As for bringing German children to Palestine, all that's going to happen is that the Labor Party will get hold of them and make Bolsheviks out of them."

"They're in danger," Henrietta said. "The regime in Germany has ordered discrimination against the Jews in every area. Our brothers and sisters are losing their jobs. Their children are subject to insults."

"So were my parents," the head of the committee replied

bitterly. "Let the spoiled rich Germans wrest their livelihood from the desert the way we did."

Henrietta sighed in despair. It was not the first time she had encountered closed minds.

The situation of the German Jews grew steadily worse. She wrote to her sisters, "Extending help to the Jews in Germany is like carrying water in a sieve. The throttling process is the most inconceivably refined torture ever heard of." By this she meant the German discrimination in all areas that was squeezing the Jews from jobs and schools and from all their normal pursuits. "And yet," she went on, "some Jews in Germany have set themselves to adjusting, going back to the Middle Ages when Jews were not allowed any occupation but petty trading and had to live in ghettoes."

Bertha came to Palestine to visit, hoping to bring Henrietta back to the United States with her. But Henrietta couldn't leave yet; the needs of the German Jews were too pressing.

She got no satisfaction from this work. It was not like building a hospital, something creative. This was a dreary rescue job made necessary by the unreasonable malice of men. Henrietta wrote on September 29, 1933, "Somehow or other I have lost the harmoniousness of living, of which I used to boast to myself."

Finally, Recha Freier's pleas were recognized. Henrietta, along with Arthur Ruppin, was assigned by the Jewish Agency to make plans for the immigration of German youth.

Recha Freier came to Palestine to meet with them. "You have no idea of the hostile atmosphere existing in Germany," she said. "It's as if our friends and neighbors had suddenly turned crazy."

Henrietta's heart was heavy. Fighting against the Germans in World War I had been sad for her, but to have cultured, intelligent Germans turn against the Jews, who had always been such proud citizens of Germany, was intolerable.

Bringing German children to Palestine would not be easy.

"You know, the British mandatory government has restricted immigration," she told Recha.

"A fine time to restrict," said Recha bitterly.

"There is a way." Henrietta pondered. "If a limited number of children come without parents to stay at a youth village, they can get special certificates."

"Good, good," said Recha.

"There is only one trouble." Henrietta sighed. "We have exactly one youth village, Ben-Schemen, run by a man named Siegfried Lehmann. He has been bringing in some Zionist teenagers for a year. But one settlement can't begin to handle all the youngsters who have to come."

As places to receive children were sought in Palestine, Henrietta traveled to Berlin in November 1933 to meet with the people who were trying to organize the youth immigration. They called their movement Jugendaliyah, which meant Youth Aliyah or Coming Up of the Youth.

The parents of the young people were in an agony of indecision. Should they send their children away or let them stay in a country that was growing daily more uncomfortable for them? Many still clung to the hope that the Nazi nightmare was only temporary.

They said, "You want our children to go to crude settlements with no modern conveniences. How can they adjust? They have never been away from home. They will be so far from us!"

Henrietta listened patiently, aware of the real difficulties the parents were describing. Yes, it was true. These teenagers had been brought up in comfortable middle-class environments. They were unprepared for pioneer life in Palestine.

There was but one solution: prepare the children before they left, gradually get them used to a rough life and lack of privacy in camps before sending them to Palestine.

A school run by the Youth Aliyah organization was established in Berlin for those teenagers who wished to go to Palestine. They learned agricultural skills and Hebrew, as well as regular high school subjects. Most of all, they learned how to live independently of their parents and to cooperate with a group.

Although the teenagers were nervous about going to Palestine, they also knew that to stay in a country where hatred was shouted at them every day and where they could have no hope for an education or a decent job was something they could not face. In many cases, they showed more courage than their parents.

Germany was rapidly becoming a police state. Like many insane people, the Nazis began seeing reflections of themselves everywhere. Everyone was an enemy, a threat to their existence. They began monitoring telephone calls, watching every move citizens made. A new agency, the Gestapo, secret police, was established to protect the regime. Soon rumors of dreadful tortures inflicted by the Gestapo circulated and the people walked around numb with fear. Meanwhile the Jew-hate and rantings of Der Führer, or The Leader, as Hitler was called, became more and more violent.

German Jews had no trouble leaving Germany; the Nazis were glad to see them go. But they had to go someplace and other countries had immigration quotas. In Palestine, the British mandatory government was also stingy about granting entrance certificates. They were afraid of offending the Arabs, whose leaders had whipped up a fear of excessive Jewish immigration.

In Germany, Recha Freier despaired at the restrictions. "We must choose the best children," she declared. "They must leave at once."

Eva Stern, a young woman who had taken over much of the administrative work of Youth Aliyah in Berlin, reminded her, "You can't just ship children to Palestine. Places have to be prepared for them there, more youth camps or room in the kibbutzim." Her eyes stung with tears as she thought of the precious children and the few certificates available. "And we can't play God and choose one child over the other."

It was decided to open the Youth Aliyah schools in Germany to all teenagers between the ages of twelve and seventeen. At least the children would get an education, now either denied to them in regular schools or offered along with degrading insults. As they passed through the rigors of training, some youngsters themselves would decide that the pioneer life was not for them or that they didn't want to go so far from home. Hopefully, enough immigration certificates would be found for those remaining.

In Palestine, there were no longer people in orange groves debating whether or not to help the Germans. News of the Nazi terror had penetrated to the most remote settlements. Kibbutzniks were all clamoring to take children. There was some politics involved too. Every kibbutz had its own philosophy, and each felt that by enlarging its ranks with the teenagers it would have more power in the country.

By 1934, groups of trained Youth Aliyah teenagers began to come to Palestine. Henrietta received word that a group of sixteen boys and girls, destined for Mishmar Ha-Emek settlement, was due to arrive.

Arrangements had been made for the reception of the young people, but Henrietta wanted to make very sure everything was perfect. "After all, these are my children," she said, and took a trip to the kibbutz.

At the kibbutz she had a conference with the administrators, who belonged to a group interested in education, called Shomer Ha-Zair. They seemed ideal to take over the responsibility for the teenagers.

The kibbutz itself was beautiful. Henrietta walked over the length and breadth of it, admiring the newly forested hill, the anemones and yellow asphodel carpeting the meadows. The school administrator marched beside her, trying to keep up with the brisk walk of the seventy-three-year-old lady.

Henrietta stopped abruptly and pointed. "Those pools are mosquito breeders. Do you want the children to get malaria? They must be drained."

The administrator stopped smiling and wrote in his note-book.

When they reached the quarters where the young people were to live, Henrietta prowled in and out. She returned and glared at the administrator. "Youth Aliyah is paying you to take care of these young people. As part of the agreement you were to provide hot showers in the washhouse. Where are the showers?"

The administrator trembled under her steady gaze. "Well, you know, there is a shortage of labor. We didn't have the materials. The showers will be built."

"I'll guarantee you those showers will be installed," she snapped. "Because I am not moving from this spot until I see it done. My children are arriving tomorrow."

And the elegant old lady in her neat gray suit, with her hat tidily set upon her head and secured with a rubber band under the smooth bun of gray hair, stayed at the wash-house and watched as the workmen installed the show-ers.

After that incident, kibbutzim who were to receive Youth Aliyah children were careful to make sure the accommoda-tions were what they were supposed to be. One never knew when the fussy old lady with the riveting brown-eyed stare was going to show up.

For her part, Henrietta welcomed these outings to rural outposts to inspect Youth Aliyah camps. She wrote to her sister Adele's husband, Thomas Seltzer, on February 1, 1935, "Fortunately for me, the administration of the German Youth Immigration brings me in closer touch than I have ever been before with the rural population, in particular with the co-operative settlements into which the youth groups are in-corporated. Even there one finds much that might be better. But also one has the feeling that it *will* be better.

"With the imperfections, it is beautiful, the promise of a better order of things. There prevails such fineness and depth of understanding of life and its claims that one goes away from contact with it with the assurance that man is a perfectable creature.

"I have to discuss many problems with the leaders of the cooperative settlements, the sort of problems attached to the adolescent human. From such discussions I always come away stimulated and elevated. These contacts with a Messianic trend of thought and living are my compensation for the hours [spent considering] the seamy side of life kept before my eyes by my social service undertakings."

When the Youth Aliyah teenagers bound for Mishmar Ha-Emek came down the gangplank of their ship in Haifa carrying their meager belongings, Henrietta was there. "I am your *ima*, your mother, in Palestine," she said and gave each of them a hug and a kiss. After all, that is what a mother is supposed to do when her children come home. Then she got into the bus with them and accompanied them to the settlement.

She learned the names of each child, and as she left, she said to them, "You know I am here. Write to me and let me know how you are getting along. Tell me your troubles. I am your mother."

The teenagers sitting on their bunks in this strange place were comforted. Some had left their parents with heartbreaking farewells, not knowing what was going to happen to them. Others had seen their parents arrested and sent to concentration camps, to disappear forever.

But there was someone in this new land who cared for them. True, she was older than some of their grandmothers, but her eyes were young. It seemed, speaking to her, that she was also a teenager, a much wiser teenager than they, and they could say anything they wanted to her.

Riding back to Jerusalem, Henrietta couldn't help smiling. Here she had grieved for so long because she had no children and now, suddenly, she had sixteen. God willing, there would be hundreds of others.

It occurred to her that motherhood involved something

more than a hug and a kiss. Each of the teenagers was an individual and many would have problems.

She squared her shoulders. Problems were what made this stubborn, caring lady thrive.

In the settlements, Youth Aliyah teenagers lived in neat bungalows. They studied for half a day and worked on the kibbutz the rest of the day.

The first job was for everyone to know Hebrew fluently. "It took only about three months for most of us to learn the language," recalled Joe Mohr, a former Youth Aliyah student who eventually came to the United States. Along with his brother, Joe went to Kibbutz Yehuda Blum in 1943, much later than most Youth Aliyah students. With his parents, he had come from Czechoslovakia via a long frightening journey. For a time they had been in the Bergen-Belsen death camp, but all miraculously survived. Occasionally, but not often, Nazis permitted groups of Jews to be ransomed through large sums of money sent by organizations and wealthy Jews, mainly from the United States. This ransom money, of course, lined the pockets of influential Nazis. A man named Adolf Eichmann, who was responsible for the deaths of many Jews and was finally hanged in Israel, sometimes took these bribes. Often Nazis pocketed the money and sent the Jews to the death camps anyway.

The Mohr family were part of a group that actually got to Palestine during World War II.

Joe and his brother were among the very few Youth Aliyah students who had parents living nearby. "It's a funny thing," he remembers, "when you got to know the kids you could ask them anything, but no one ever asked, 'Who are your parents?' For too many kids, the question was painful, so we avoided it altogether."

Those parents who reached Palestine sometimes gave Henrietta a hard time. They demanded her attention and were critical of Youth Aliyah. But, realizing that they had been through violent experiences and changes that made them crabby and unreasonable, she listened patiently, if wearily.

She wrote to her sisters, "The Youth Immigration drives me constantly from my desk. I am always chasing after a child or welcoming them or investigating a place for them. I rush so fast I can't think."

She was interrupted at her letter writing by yet another telephone call. "The British have changed the rules again. They had allotted certificates to youth up to the age of seventeen. Now, like a thunderclap, they've decided to grant them only up to age sixteen. Dozens of boys and girls seventeen years old have completed their training and are waiting in Germany. What will we do?"

"It will work out," she forced herself to say.

But irritation at the authorities tasted like metal in her mouth. How could they behave so capriciously? She knew exactly the number of overage waiting teenagers—255—and they were a month late in arriving.

The phone rang, this time from a Youth Aliyah camp in Degania. "We have a child here with scarlet fever. What shall we do?"

"Bring him to the isolation hospital in Jerusalem, of course."

Henrietta was not without eager helpers. They swarmed around, each with a pet project too impractical to put into effect even if the funds were available, which they were not. The most irritating were some American tourists who not only took up her precious time, but were free with advice. In a letter home she described a typical tourist: "He is stupid, uninformed, hasty in judgment, has pettifogging intervals, won't let you either praise or criticize or even analyze. And if he stays only two days he possesses all these qualities to the nth degree."

In March 1935, twenty boys and girls arrived to join others already at Kibbutz Gevah. As the new students marched in, each girl and boy carried a young sapling. Ceremoniously, they knelt and planted their trees, the act symbolizing their union with the soil of Palestine.

Ima dances with Youth Aliyah children.

One place in the row of trees had been left vacant.

"It's for you, Ima," they cried.

Solemnly, Henrietta carried her sapling to the empty place and planted it.

A shout went up from both the veterans and the newcomers. Then followed a celebration of singing and dancing as the older students welcomed their younger brothers and sisters, cleansing away, for a time, the homesickness and fear.

10

Ima

Henrietta was not content just to meet the young people at the boat. She traveled throughout the country visiting them.

One group had settled in Tel Hai. Calling themselves a *plugah,* "training group," they were preparing to start a new settlement in the Huleh area of the upper Galilee. Tel Hai was well known as the place where the hero Trumpeldor had died defending it from a Bedouin attack with the words "It is good to die for our country" on his lips. Now young people were prepared to live for their country.

Henrietta brushed aside the administrator's invitation to tea in the comfort of the dining room. "Later," she said and strode off toward the chicken yard.

"Ima, Ima," called a voice over the cackle of hens. A young girl with rosy cheeks and copper-colored braids swinging under a flowered kerchief ran up to her. She threw her arms around Henrietta, surrounding her with the odor of the chicken yard and the smell of healthy young sweat.

Chatting with young men at a Youth Aliyah camp

"How brown you have become, Clara. A child of the sun."

"A child of the chicken yard, rather." Clara laughed. There was a special light in her blue eyes. Clara would have a secret to tell.

"Come, sit down, Ima." Clara upended a wooden crate and brushed it off. "Enjoy the sun."

Henrietta sat down and Clara perched in front of her. "Do you like chickens?" Henrietta asked.

"I do. I do. They are like little children. I love to see the tiny chicks grow." Clara raised her voice above the cackle of the barnyard.

"I don't mind the noise," remarked Henrietta. "I'm used to hens. When I go to America I am surrounded by them. They call themselves Hadassah ladies."

Clara giggled.

"We mustn't speak that way about the good women who've worked so hard to raise money for Youth Aliyah," Henrietta said, partly to soothe the pang that her mention of America had raised. There was no way now to get home; she could not be spared from her work.

Clara grew quiet. Henrietta sensed homesickness in her too.

"Have you had word from your parents, Clara? In Darmstadt, aren't they?"

"Ima, how do you remember such things? You know everything about us. Yes." She sighed. "Times are very hard for them, but they managed to send me some art materials."

"Good." Henrietta smiled. "It's all very well for you to be queen of the chicken coops, but you mustn't neglect your gifts. I understand that you are teaching drawing and painting to the children of Kfar Gilead. That is important work. We mustn't forget that although life in this country can be rough, there's beauty too. The children have to experience that."

Clara stood up and stared at the blue haze of the distant hills. "Ima," she said slowly, "do you think there is a chance my parents can come to Palestine? I get so frightened, thinking of them in Germany."

Henrietta felt as if a fist were closing in her chest. This was the question she heard over and over, yet there was little hope. Not only had the British restricted immigration into Palestine, but quotas for Jews fleeing Germany were small in other countries as well. Most German Jews were trapped, with nowhere to go.

But she said, "Perhaps." After all, who knew?

Now she turned the girl's face to her own. "Clara, there is something in your eyes, something you have to tell me. You can't fool this old lady, you know."

Red spread from Clara's neck up to her forehead.

"Is there someone?"

"Yes."

"What is his name?"

"Gideon." Clara's face was transfigured with joy, as if the name of Gideon had the sound of angels playing harps.

"It's serious, I see, for you. And for him?"

"Gideon wants to marry me."

Clara's joy was too precious to spoil with words of caution and yet Henrietta thought of the mother trapped in faraway Darmstadt, Germany. "I must meet Gideon, just as your own parents would wish to, and give my consent."

This was a new chore Henrietta had undertaken, investigating the men some of the older Youth Aliyah girls wanted to marry. Parents wrote to her and insisted upon it, and Henrietta was willing to comply. However, sometimes when she wasn't sure the marriage was a good idea, the couple married anyway. And then the parents in Germany fretted and were angry with her. Fortunately, in this case, she liked the sturdy young farmer, Gideon. Later, when Clara and Gideon were married, they joined the group that was settling the Huleh and draining the swamps.

Back at the administrative building, the director greeted Henrietta with tea and cake and a report of a problem child.

"Harry is the son of a wealthy textile manufacturer," the director read. "His parents are now in Spain."

Henrietta listened, her chin in her hand. She was tired, but it was important to know about Harry. "He is not adjusting?" she asked. "He looks like a strong boy to me. And he was very enthusiastic about farm life."

The director sighed. "The question of what goes on in a child's mind is very complicated."

Henrietta smiled. This was hardly news.

The director went on. "Harry is used to a pampered life. It's too rugged for him here. He can't keep up. He's having difficulty in his studies too, can't seem to concentrate." His fingers drummed on the tabletop. "Perhaps the boy is homesick."

"They are all homesick," said Henrietta, wishing to add, "We are all homesick." She thought for a moment about Harry. "I think," she said, "the best thing to do is to let the boy develop at his own pace. Don't pressure him. Praise him for his successes and minimize his lacks. When he feels more confident about himself, he will work better."

A trickle of Zionist youth from organizations like Masada, an American youth group, was beginning to come to Palestine. Unlike the Germans, if conditions were too hard, or they were too homesick, they were free to return home. Frequently, that is what they did.

Among the young people who came were Henrietta's nephew Benjamin Levin and his wife, Sarah. They settled into a kibbutz called Rodges. As soon as she could, Henrietta made time to visit them.

Sarah came to the door of their little bungalow. "Benjamin is off picking oranges, Aunt Henrietta. It is quite far away, so he couldn't get back to see you."

"So, the more chance I will have to visit with you, woman to woman." Henrietta smiled to hide her disappointment. The dream of her life was to have family close by and now that, miraculously, her beloved nephew was right here in Palestine, they had practically no time to see each other.

Sarah ushered her into the little room that served as a living room, bedroom, and kitchen, the latter consisting of a hot plate sent from America.

Henrietta seated herself on a rough homemade sofa covered a bit crookedly with a hand-sewn flowered slipcover. At the window was a matching curtain, also a little crooked. But there were plants in the windows and books on the shelves.

"You've made your home cosy," Henrietta commented.

"Almost cosy," said Sarah, returning from the hot plate with a pot of tea. She brought over an orange crate table and put out a pair of tin cups.

Henrietta looked at her niece's earnest face and her faded

gingham dress. Life on the kibbutz was very different from back home. "So you are both working hard."

Sarah spread out her roughened hands. "I'm doing my share. I was given time off to meet with you. Benjamin works so hard, he goes right to sleep as soon as he gets home. We have no chance at all to participate in the social life of the kibbutz."

Henrietta listened to Sarah's complaints without comment. Much as she loved him, she knew her Benjamin. When things got hard, he quit. This couple was not long for Palestine, she thought.

That was one of the few times in her life that Henrietta was wrong. Benjamin and Sarah left the kibbutz and made a few other changes, but they finally settled down successfully in Palestine.

A few days after the visit, Henrietta was busy as usual, burrowing through mountains of paperwork, when her assistant peered through the doorway of her office. "I think you'd better come down to the reception room."

Henrietta followed the assistant down the hall to the outer office. There she found an immigration official and a very dirty and very thin boy about thirteen years old. "Captain of a freighter found him a stowaway, ma'am," said the official. "He turned him over to us and we were told to bring him to you."

The boy jerked away from the official's hand on his shoulder and hobbled to the other side of the room. One of his legs was cruelly twisted. He wore a tattered man's jacket and pants that were more holes than fabric, all so grimy one could not see the original color. His hair, a jungle of dark matted curls, hung below his ears and down his neck and partially covered his greenish eyes, which glinted with wary suspicion. The boy's back was bent a little and his hands with their broken, blackened fingernails moved automatically before his face in the stance of one who has been cornered yet is determined to claw his way out of the trap.

"Leave him to me," Henrietta told the official. "You did well to bring him here." To the boy, she beckoned and tried a smile. He remained rigid.

"Come," she said, first in Hebrew. Then she tried Yiddish and he moved unwillingly after her.

She sat in her office, the boy in front of her, and studied him. The smell of unwashed days at sea, of the filth of a ship, of a thousand unnamable things, filled the room. She was thankful that the window was open to warm May breezes.

"What is your name?" she asked in Yiddish.

"Isaac. I am a Zionist."

Henrietta smiled, but not in derision. He was such a small Zionist. "Good," she said. "Eretz Israel needs all the Zionists it can get. How old are you, Isaac?"

"Thirteen."

"And your parents? Where are they?"

He shrugged. "Dead. When I was little."

"And your home?"

"Lodz, in Poland."

"That is very far away. How did you get here?"

Isaac told Henrietta a story that seemed impossible to believe; yet here he was, a Polish boy in Palestine. Lame leg and all, he had walked all across Europe, scuttling past borders until he reached Costanza, Turkey. There he stole aboard a steamer bound for Palestine, but was discovered. He ran off the ship and hid until he was able to stow away again. He did this three times. Finally, he remained hidden on a freighter until the ship reached Palestine. Just as he was about to jump off the ship, he was caught.

The captain turned him over to immigration officials, who were about to send him back. But they didn't quite know where to send him. He was not Turkish, so they couldn't return him to Costanza, and it would have been impossible to get him back to Poland. The immigration people contacted a Jewish official, who assured them that the community would take care of the boy and that he would not become a burden.

Henrietta smiled wryly. By community, the official had meant Henrietta Szold. Who else?

She reached over and placed his twisted leg upon her spotless skirt, pulled up the torn pants, and stroked the leg. "How did you get this?"

"A sickness. Polio. When I was a baby. The walking made it worse." He winced as she kneaded the muscles, probing to find the extent of the damage.

"Is it painful?"

He pressed his lips together. "No," he said, but the sound came out strangled. Suddenly he brushed his eyes with the back of a dirty hand and started to sniff. Gently, Henrietta put the leg down and gave him a clean white handkerchief. "My, you have a cold."

He nodded rapidly. After all, he was a man. He had walked across Europe. And men don't cry.

"Isaac, we have a hospital called the Hadassah Hospital. We have very good doctors. Perhaps a doctor can help your leg. First you and I will have a very fine lunch and then we will go to the hospital."

The Hadassah doctors operated on Isaac's leg three times and they said that, even though it was not perfect, at least he would have much better use of it. They were very pleased.

Henrietta went often to visit the boy. Clean, and with some good food inside him and his curls cut close, "he looked like an angel, a little Jewish angel," she told her friends.

Isaac liked to play chess, sometimes by himself, but there was something he liked to do even better. He told Henrietta he liked to sculpt and she brought him clay. He created beautiful animals and figures. She was immensely proud of him, he was so clever and talented.

But one day when Isaac was nearly healed from his last operation and almost ready to go to a Youth Aliyah camp, Henrietta came to the hospital and found his bed empty.

"We don't know what happened to him, Miss Szold," said a nurse. "The night nurse left him and went on her rounds, and when she returned, he was gone. He had taken his clothes and some of that clay you brought him. But he did leave this."

She handed Henrietta a beautifully modeled figure of a man with a beard. Henrietta held the little figure lovingly in her hands and said sadly, "No matter how much we loved him, he just couldn't trust us. He probably thought we were fooling him, getting his confidence and then we'd betray him and send him back to Poland. And he'd been through too much to risk that."

Actually, Isaac knew that his status had not been cleared by immigration authorities. The Jewish community would do everything it could to protect him, but he wasn't taking any chances.

Henrietta left the hospital carrying the little figure. As she went down the steps, she looked at a riot of pink and red roses climbing all over a fence. This cheered her. "It will be all right. Isaac is safe at home. He's clever and he will do well."

11

"We Are Facing Gigantic Tasks!"

In the fall of 1935, Henrietta went for an extended trip. First she visited relatives in Vienna, then she went to the Congress of World Zionists in Zurich, Switzerland. After that, she journeyed to Amsterdam to a meeting of those involved in Youth Aliyah. Finally, she visited Germany.

She addressed the Zionist Congress in Zurich, describing the work of Youth Aliyah and the efforts to aid other German immigrants to Palestine. The Congress voted her two-thirds of the funding she asked for. Accustomed to short funding, Henrietta was satisfied. She started for her seat but, to her surprise, was motioned back to the podium.

A representative of the German delegation came to the microphone. "In recognition of the aid Henrietta Szold has given to our children, the German delegation has an honor they wish to bestow upon her."

Henrietta was touched. With all their troubles, the German Jews had taken the effort to give her an award, probably

Reporting on the Youth Aliyah program in Switzerland. *Seated far left:* Chaim Weizmann.

another plaque to add to her collection. But then came an announcement that, as she later wrote to her sisters, paralyzed her with surprise.

"The German immigrants to Palestine have decided to name a new settlement Kfar Szold, in honor of Henrietta Szold. Her name will be perpetuated as long as that settlement shall last."

Henrietta faced the delegation, thanking them, her eyes filled with tears and her throat clogged with emotion. Their clothing was threadbare, their faces drawn and anxious, yet they were trying to carry on normal lives in spite of the terrible plague of Nazism that had infected their homeland.

After the Zurich meeting she went to Amsterdam, where she met Youth Aliyah fundraiser Ilse Warburg, youth leader Bertha Pappenheim, Eva Stern, administrative head of Youth Aliyah in Berlin, and others working for Youth Aliyah. It was still possible for German Jews to travel, but they had to return to Germany because immigration visas were scarce and there was no way for them to stay permanently in other countries.

Henrietta was particularly drawn to young Eva Stern, possibly because there was an American connection. Eva's father, a child psychologist, was a professor at a college in North Carolina.

"There is no reason for you to stay in Germany," Henrietta urged her. "Surely your father has influential friends who can get you into the United States to stay with your parents."

Eva smiled wistfully, but there was an air of strength beneath the young curves of her face. "Those of us working with children have made a pact. We will not leave as long as there are children to be saved." She made a ghost of a joke. "Sort of like a captain not leaving his ship."

"Besides," Eva added, "I have made a friend, a very close friend, Dolph Michaelis. He is also a youth worker. I would not leave Dolph."

Henrietta looked into her young friend's eyes, celebrating the birth of love amid all the hate.

Just at that moment, Bertha Pappenheim, a large, formidable-looking woman who had been hovering nearby, came up to Henrietta. With a movement of her hand, she dismissed Eva. "I wish to speak to Miss Szold alone."

Henrietta was offended by the woman's rudeness, but she was totally unprepared for what came next. Her eyes blazing with anger, Mrs. Pappenheim hissed, "What do you think you are doing? You are crucifying our children, taking them to Palestine. These are German children and they belong in Germany with their families. You will never get one of the children in my charge to go to Youth Aliyah."

Henrietta couldn't believe her ears. How could Bertha Pappenheim feel this way? Didn't she see the storm clouds over Germany getting blacker and blacker? Didn't she want children to have a normal life?

With difficulty, she resisted the impulse to yell back at Mrs. Pappenheim. All she could say was that she had no intentions toward the children under Mrs. Pappenheim's charge. "Youth Aliyah has enough trouble getting entrance certificates for those who want to come. Of course, if in the future you or your charges change your minds, we'll do our best to help you."

"Never," said Bertha.

Several years later, Henrietta learned that Bertha Pappenheim and the children for whom she was responsible had all perished in a concentration camp.

Following the meeting in Amsterdam, Henrietta went to Berlin. Except for groups of brown-shirted storm troopers walking around the city, everything seemed normal. The stores were open and transportation moved, and there was entertainment. Even the Jews, with strained faces and eyes darting in every direction lest someone overhear them and arrest them for some unknown crime, were clinging to a regular life. The Jewish organizations had pooled their meager resources to plan a big celebration in her honor.

When Henrietta entered her hotel, she noticed a peculiar hush. All the guests and staff were huddled near radios, listening to a blast of martial music. This was followed by an official announcement:

"The following laws have been established at Nuremberg. One: All Jews are henceforth non-citizens. They are forbidden to show the German flag. Two: Jews are prohibited from marrying non-Jews. Three: Jews are forbidden to employ German servants. A Jew is defined as a person with at least one Jewish grandparent."

Tears rolled down Henrietta's cheeks as she unpacked. The proud German Jews, so conscious of their German culture,

Henrietta, *second from left*, talking with Emma Ehrlich, aboard ship, 1935

an important part of the nation for generations, were now reduced to being non-citizens. Some Germans who didn't even know they were Jews were also included in the Nuremberg Laws. And there were people married to non-Jews, who loved them very much. What would happen to those marriages?

Two weeks later, back in Palestine, she put her feelings and experiences into a letter written to Bertha and Adele on October 10, 1935.

"I hardly know how to approach the Berlin chapter of my

European trip. Ever since leaving Berlin, I've been trying to find a summarizing formula for my experiences and impressions. They are too numerous for a single summation. Yet I am sure that a thinker of vision could put the situation and the reaction to it on the part of the German Jews into a striking sentence that would convey the woe, the dignity, the throttling pain, the astonishment of the beholder that such things can be, the dumb despair when amazement gives room for thought, the rebellious temper that succeeds amazement and thought at the beastly logic of the Hitlerite.

"I entered Berlin at the very moment almost at which Hitler was delivering his speech at Nuremberg in which the new legislation was announced. More or less the Nazi intentions were known before. But with the saving grace of humanity, one hopes up to the last moment that the worst will not happen.

"I knew that in Berlin all sorts of preparations had been made to press the most out of my visit for the good of the propaganda for the Youth Immigration; and I could not bear the thought of the public demonstrations which had been intended for the following week and were now going to be kept to the letter though the dreaded blow had fallen.

"The Jewish organizations went through with the program with grim determination. They used each of my public appearances as an occasion to assert their undaunted courage in the face of the degradation inflicted upon them and to announce plans chiefly of an educational character, to remove the sting from the persecution and maintain the cultural standard of former days at least in dealing with their young people."

The chief problem in educating German Jewish children at that time was at the junior high school level, for young people between the ages of fourteen and sixteen. Hopefully, at sixteen they would be eligible to go to Palestine with Youth Aliyah.

Henrietta's letter described the situation of teenagers between fourteen and sixteen. "The boys and girls are left totally without occupation and without hope during those two or three years. I cannot begin to describe to you what indignities they are exposed to, not so much in the large cities as in the small towns.

"In the populous centers, like Berlin and Hamburg, the Jews are living as it were anonymously. They are affected, of course, by the legislation, but less by the malice of the Nazi madmen. In the small towns every Jew is known and Nazi persecution spins more.

"While I was in Germany the Jews in Berlin had to send milk and bread to the small places all over the Reich, but principally in the northeast, the Nazis having forbidden food sellers to dispose of their wares to Jews. Little children were starving.

"A short time before I got there, a small orphanage with thirty-five inmates was told by a Nazi horde at ten o'clock at night that by a half hour after midnight the building was needed by them and would therefore have to be vacated permanently by that time. An appeal to the circuit authorities was of no avail. The children, aged from five to sixteen, had to be removed hurriedly to a Frankfurt institution."

Even so, the meetings in Henrietta's honor were held. The first evening she met with a group of one hundred twenty-five persons, the ones who had originated the idea of a village to bear her name. After the introductory address, the main speaker, a Mr. Seeligsohn, proceeded with a subject that swept Henrietta off her feet with surprise. The man was talking about her father! He recalled a birthday commemoration service in honor of Moses Mendelssohn (a learned rabbi, grandfather of Felix Mendelssohn, the composer). The main speaker had been Rabbi Szold.

Henrietta wrote to her sisters: "The speaker then proceeded to analyze the address our father delivered and used it to demonstrate the love of the Jew for German literature, German language, the German people, his identification with them." The reason for Mr. Seeligsohn's choice of material was to link Henrietta and her work with those things that had been close to her father's heart. She was intensely touched.

She went on to describe the rest of the excitement that had been caused by her presence in Berlin: "My reception was nothing short of homage. Even the little children know me.

"Another meeting that I should like to describe is the one with the parents of the boys and girls—seven hundred fifty of them—under my charge in Palestine. Can you imagine my consternation when I entered a hall packed with eight hundred persons, with whom I was to have an intimate conversation about their children?" Henrietta thought of a solution. She told the parents that the only children she knew intimately were those who were problems. Of course, this did not refer to any of their youngsters!

When Henrietta finished her business in Berlin, she decided to visit Youth Aliyah camps throughout Germany. As she traveled to Silesia, everywhere she saw Nazi hatred. Stretched across the main road were signs, JUDEN NICHT ERWÜNSCHT (JEWS NOT WANTED) and MÄDCHEN UND FRAUEN, JUDEN SIND VERDERBER (GIRLS AND WOMEN, JEWS ARE YOUR CORRUPTERS).

Once, while speaking to parents of Youth Aliyah children in a small town, she heard marching storm troopers outside in the street yelling, "*Jude, verrecke!* (Jews, perish from the earth!)" She looked out over the shabby auditorium, with its faded draperies and worn seats, at the small group of men and women, equally shabby, equally worn, and she wanted to cry. But they were not weeping, even though their neighbors wanted them to perish. They were beyond anguish; they were sending their children away.

Henrietta steadied herself and continued speaking as if nothing was happening. These people needed to know that

Germany was not the world; outside, children still studied and played without fear.

Depressed, she wrote home: "So far as the Jews in Germany are concerned, in less than twenty-five years not one will be left. The older ones will have died and the others will have been forced out, some to be destroyed in their wanderings, a small percentage to be established in Palestine, if there are means!"

Discouraged as she was, she had no inkling that the worst was to come. The Nazi death camps had not yet been put into full operation.

When Henrietta returned to Berlin, there was horrified talk of the arrest of Dr. Leo Baeck, the chief rabbi of Berlin and main spokesman for the Jewish people. Dr. Baeck had been detained for a few hours because, in defiance of the Nazis, he had written a message of hope and courage to be read in eight hundred synagogues on Yom Kippur Eve. The message was confiscated before it could be read, but some copies had made it to other countries; Henrietta had heard it during her visit to Austria. She described it as "a noble, touching document, a true reflex of the nobility and dignity of the German Jews in this day of their trial."

But there were some German Jews who still didn't understand the gravity of their situation. Henrietta wrote: "What they forget is that even if Hitler were removed from the scene, he would leave behind two poisoned generations, the young people and children under twenty, the future citizens who will soon sit in the seats of the legislators and the judges and social leaders, and they will act out of the consciousness of a Nazi education, without having known Jews personally."

(Fortunately, that prediction did not come true. The postwar German government was very conscious of re-educating its young, and the new generation, while perhaps not too familiar with Jews, has not expressed a poisonous attitude. In fact, the German government has made shrines of the

death camps to remind its people of the horrors of unrea-
soning hate.)

Even during the worst of the Nazi terror, there were many
Christian Germans who detested what was happening. When
Henrietta visited the home of her friends the Eskeles, in
Berlin, she experienced something that was like a message
of sanity. Mrs. Eskeles had a guest, a Christian friend who
had come from a small town to spend a few days, bringing
her ten-year-old daughter.

"I felt it is important that I come here," she said. "My little
girl is exposed to so much hatred of Jews in our town, it
makes me afraid. She needs to spend time with our dear
Jewish friends so that she won't forget to love them."

A resolution embedded itself in Henrietta's mind. She, too,
must guard against hatred. The Youth Aliyah children must
always be taught that their tragedies were caused by a few
ravening beasts who did not deserve to be called men. But
in Germany itself there were good people. Some of them
helped Jews at great danger to themselves. The young people
must know that.

Another fine Christian woman who made contact with
Henrietta was the artist Kathe Kollwitz, who sent her a copy
of one of her most famous pictures, *Mother and Child,* in honor
of the Youth Immigration movement. Speaking out against
the Nazi regime, Kathe Kollwitz would not be silenced although she was forbidden to show her work or to appear in
public.

When Henrietta came to visit her and thank her for the
lithograph, Miss Kollwitz shook her head in despair. "Hitler
will not rest until every last Jew has been hunted out of
Germany."

With a heavy heart, Henrietta returned to Palestine. In
addition to the plight of German youngsters, she heard of
difficult times for young people in Lithuania, Poland, and
France, where the children of refugees were permitted no
opportunities because they were foreigners. There were also

problems in Russian Carpathia. It would take the resources not only of Hadassah, but of the Keren Ha-Yesod and the Keren Kayemet, other fund-raising organizations, to make homes for all these children. There was but one way to put it.

Henrietta wrote: "We are facing gigantic tasks!"

12

Jacob and Esau

The cold rains of autumn 1935 pelted the earth. No matter how dreadful the weather, Henrietta insisted upon meeting every boat carrying Youth Aliyah youngsters. In spite of the protests of her secretary, Emma Ehrlich, she bundled up, wearing boots and carrying a big umbrella, and went down to Haifa driven by her faithful assistant, Hans Beyth. Hans, who recently had arrived from Germany, had been recommended to Henrietta by Eva Stern's fiancé, Dolph Michaelis.

Shortly before her seventy-fifth birthday in December 1935, Henrietta traveled to the United States. Much against her nature, for she hated being the center of a circus, she permitted Hadassah to mark the birthday with what seemed an endless number of tributes and celebrations. She was made an honorary citizen of New York, and given the key to the city. Not to be outdone, the city of Tel Aviv cabled that she was an honorary citizen of their city too. Another tribute was a forest planted in her name in Palestine by Hadassah.

Henrietta braced herself for all the unwelcome attention.

Henrietta and Hans Beyth, in suit, in garden at Ashold Yaakov

Fiorello LaGuardia, mayor of New York City, shaking hands with Henrietta at ceremony in which she was given the key to the city

"Let them do anything they want, as long as money is raised for our projects," she told her fellow Hadassah members. And, although there was a severe economic depression in the United States, the one hundred thousand women of Hadassah rallied to the cause. Desperately needed money poured in from all directions.

On a day shortly after Henrietta's return to Palestine in February, Emma Ehrlich came into her office with a concerned look on her face. "Miss Szold, I have received a call from the Social Service Training School. They have a most unusual and puzzling case and they would like your advice. Can you meet with them?"

A Jewish National Fund Project: the Henrietta Szold Forest

Henrietta was about to protest that she was much too busy, but there was a certain look in Emma's eyes; this was a request that couldn't be denied. She pushed aside the ever-present pile of papers and went with Emma over to the school.

She found the entire student body, looking remarkably scrubbed and well dressed, assembled. The director ushered Henrietta to a seat at the front of the room and, with a serious expression, took out an official-looking folder.

"This is an extremely difficult case, Miss Szold. Our subject claims to have the highest moral standards, yet she has a thousand children although she is not married. She completely disobeys all labor laws, working sixteen hours a day. What shall we do with this woman?"

The room rocked with laughter, and Henrietta guffawed along with them, realizing that the odd case was herself. "Happy belated birthday, Miss Szold!" they shouted. Someone appeared with an accordion. Chairs were pushed back and the students were soon twining around and around a delighted Henrietta in a rousing horah. A huge cake was wheeled in, and Henrietta was toasted and hugged.

Afterward, on the way back to their office, she said to Emma, "Now *that's* what I call a good birthday party."

In April 1936, the hand of the Nazi reached into Palestine itself. The Mufti of Jerusalem, Hitler's friend, instigated riots, telling his followers that Jewish immigration would bring in people who would destroy the Arab population.

The riots started in Jaffa. The Arabs cried, "The government is with us," thinking that the British restrictions on Jewish immigration meant they favored the Arabs. Nazi-inspired slogans were shouted in the streets: "Heil Hitler" and "The Jews are a gang of swindlers, a menace to all mankind." Pictures of Hitler were placed in the windows of Arab shops, and phonographs blared "Kill the Jews."

In largely Arab cities like Jaffa and Hebron, the Arabs threw bombs and sniped at Jews. Refugees from those places poured into Jerusalem and Tel Aviv. In addition to her work with Youth Aliyah, Henrietta had taken on the supervision of social services. Now the problems of people fleeing besieged cities right there in Palestine were added to those of European refugees.

But still, the children had to be attended to.

"Miss Szold, you absolutely, positively, must not go to Haifa to meet the boat," implored Emma. "There are Arab bandits throughout the country, throwing grenades at cars. They put nails and glass on the roads. It's too dangerous."

"If I perish, I perish." Henrietta shrugged. "But I must go to Haifa." Relenting at Emma's distress, she added, "Hans Beyth will go with me. And, I suppose, we'll have to let

Oscar the chauffeur carry a revolver, although those ugly things frighten me to death."

They met the boat without incident, but while traveling back to Jerusalem, they encountered a crowd of Arabs blocking the road. Oscar drew his revolver.

"No, no, Oscar." Henrietta stayed his hand.

She noticed that the people in the crowd were dressed in festive clothes and carried flowers. Opening the window, she called, "How nice you all look. What beautiful flowers."

"We are waiting for the Mufti," said a little girl.

Henrietta smiled at her. "And you look perfectly lovely. Now, would you all be kind enough to let our car go through?"

The crowd parted and the Arabs waved as Henrietta's car moved on.

Hans made a face. "Waiting for the Mufti, indeed! And you *smiled* at them."

"Maybe the man they were waiting for was ugly, but they were fine," she said.

Henrietta wrote, "Matters are not going to be mended if the alienation between us and the Arab population is emphasized."

She believed very strongly that Palestine was not only a geographical place where Jews could settle. She wanted it to be a center where the very essence of Judaism, the ideals of love and justice that she had learned from her father, would actually be lived, an example for the whole world.

Most people thought this was foolish. Arabs and Jews could never get along, they said. But there was a small group that agreed with her, including her friend Rabbi Judah Magnes and the philosopher Martin Buber. Buber, who was famous all over the world for his philosophy, "I-Thou," believed that by becoming still and listening, people could make contact with God's will. This, he felt, would also enable human beings to relate to one another correctly. The connection was between individuals and had nothing to do with differences in background.

Had not Henrietta made the Arabs wave, even as they waited for the Mufti, her enemy?

And though the Arabs were rampaging and killing people and tearing up orange trees that had been so lovingly tended, she could still write, "It is hard for us to conceive respect for Arab leaders whose battle cry is 'Sell no land to the Jews,' at the very moment at which they are negotiating with Jews for the sale of their own lands. However, even that does not excuse our being satisfied to reduce the Arab to a second-class citizen. If instead of sending a Royal Commission to 'investigate,' Great Britain would set up a body of wise men with the task of studying the racial antagonisms between Jacob and Esau and determine the thousand ways that might lead from Arab head to Jewish head and vice versa, the problem might be solved."

At last the Arab riots stopped and Palestine returned to normal. Youth Aliyah people replanted the trees that had been torn up. Some went to the desert and the swamps and to dangerous outposts guarded by watchtowers. The young people were growing up and adding to the strength of the country.

Henrietta's work continued at a mad pace. She wrote to her sisters, "I wish I could describe my crazy quilt of living and my headlong gait. I am tumbling all over myself all the time, and so is poor Emma Ehrlich. She can't stand the pace as well as I do—she looks pale and gaunt, and we both are gasping for breath to 'catch up'—that eternally unattainable ideal of mine."

In spite of her hectic schedule, Henrietta made time to visit Youth Aliyah groups. In 1937 at a kibbutz called Afikim, a young pianist gave a concert in her honor. She drowsed in her chair, lulled by strains of Mozart and Beethoven. The music created a curious mixture of pleasure and deep melancholy, a remembrance of the wonderful German musical heritage that had always been so important to her.

At Givat Haim Youth Aliyah facility with settled refugees

After the concert, the pianist, a young blond giant, came to talk to her. How very much he looks like the Nazi ideal of the Aryan, she thought bitterly.

"My name is Fritz, Ima," he said. "Did you like the music?"

"It was food for my soul. Come, Fritz, sit down and tell me all about yourself and how you learned to play so well."

Fritz straddled a chair and glanced with a smile at his work-hardened hands. "Believe it or not, I was the pampered only son of an ironware dealer in Köthen, Germany. Everything I wanted was mine—music lessons, rare foreign stamps, vacations, sports equipment." He grinned, the sort of smile that mocks but doesn't quite hide pain.

Henrietta's thoughts flew to the parents in Germany who had not seen their son in three years, who had no idea of the glorious man he was becoming.

"And your parents," she said gently. She had learned that

it was best to let wounds out into the air instead of pretending to cover up. "Did they object to your coming?"

He laughed, unsuccessfully. "You know parents. An only son. So protected, so unused to hardship. How will he ever survive in the Palestine wilderness?"

He reached into a pocket and brought out a photograph of himself. "Ima, I know you are going to Germany soon and will meet with parents. If you see my mother and father, will you give them this photo?"

"Of course," she said, tucking the picture into her handbag. She would add it to the hundreds she had already collected. "Now, so that I can tell your parents, what are your plans, Fritz? Are you going to concentrate on music?"

"No, Ima, music is just for fun. I'm going to be a fisherman. I've already been approved by the Jewish Agency to become a worker on the clipper *Bikura*. It's a hard life, but I am a strong man."

Henrietta gazed at his muscular physique with the admiration of a teenager. "That's wonderful," she said. "Your parents will be proud."

He scratched an ear. "I don't know. I don't think that was what they had in mind. A fisherman!"

Before going to Germany, Henrietta attended the 1937 Zionist Congress in Zurich. The delegates were chiefly concerned with a British proposal to divide Palestine into Jewish and Arab countries. Most of the delegates were in favor of an all-Jewish state, but Henrietta felt strongly that Jews and Arabs should live together in peace.

She prepared a report, which she planned to offer to the Congress: "I too, believe the land will be ours, but the way to win it is not by might and not by cunning but by the spirit of the Lord, which is the way of conciliation. This separate Jewish state that is offered means war."

But she never delivered her statement. Sensing the mood

of the delegates, she knew her words would be tossed into the wind. They had no interest in what she had to say.

Following the Congress, there was a meeting of Youth Aliyah workers, including Eva Stern.

"I wish you would come to Palestine," Henrietta begged her. "You and Dolph together." Henrietta worried constantly about the young woman for whom she felt a deep affection.

"Not yet," said Eva. "The work is not yet done." Things were getting very difficult. She told of increased harassment. "The Gestapo, the secret police, raided our office. They took all our money. They're very suspicious of Youth Aliyah, they think it's bad propaganda. After all," she said bitterly, "why would young people want to leave the glorious Reich? In order to come to this meeting, we had to lie when we applied for passports, telling them we were going to a labor congress."

Eva had brought with her some brochures describing the work of Youth Aliyah.

"How did these pass the censor?" Henrietta wanted to know.

Eva's hand flew to her mouth in mock horror. "My goodness, we completely forgot to submit them."

Henrietta gazed at her, trying not to show how frightened she was for her friend. Eva was playing with fire; but Henrietta said nothing.

Henrietta returned to Palestine and Eva to Berlin. One morning, Eva received a telephone call. "This is Herr Müller calling. I am an associate of Adolf Eichmann." Eva's heart nearly stopped. Eichmann, the butcher of the Gestapo, the man who herded Jews into death camps!

"My job," said Herr Müller, with silky smoothness, "is to investigate Jewish leaders. And you, my dear Fraulein Stern, are certainly a leader of young people." His voice took on a menacing chill. "You are to come to the police station right away."

Trembling, Eva tidied up her desk. Her secretary was rigid with fear. Eva told her, "You are to meet me at the café in an hour. If I do not come, don't be alarmed. It will mean that the police have me and are investigating. You are to inform the Youth Aliyah people."

When Eva reached the police station, she was sent to the cellar to wait. It was very dark there, illuminated by a tiny light, which shone on a sign: "INHALE DEEPLY. DON'T BE NERVOUS." This was the Nazi idea of a joke. Anyone held by the Gestapo was terrified.

However, Eva did try to breathe deeply. The air was so heavy and stale, it entered her lungs feeling like some metallic substance. The taste of it crept up her throat and settled gummily in her mouth. She could hear her own heart beating loudly. That was the only sound in the dark, thick silence.

She knew why she had been put in this place. This was a preview, a sample, of the kind of cell into which she could be put if the Gestapo was displeased with her.

Finally an officer came down and got her. He brought her to an office. The sudden light made Eva blink. Her eyes focused on a heavy man with a red jowly face and close-cropped brown hair.

"Sit down," he ordered.

She perched on the edge of a chair, telling herself that this was a good sign. Representatives of the Gestapo didn't usually ask people to sit.

"My name is Kuchmann." He leaned back in his chair and looked at her with mocking amusement. "I understand that you have recently taken a trip to Zurich."

"Yes, Herr Kuchmann." She noticed that her fingers were creasing and uncreasing her skirt, and she stopped.

"To a labor conference?"

"Yes, Herr Kuchmann," she said faintly. He knew otherwise.

He reached into a folder on his desk and brought out a

Youth Aliyah brochure and flung it on the desk before her. "Was this your labor conference?"

She nodded.

"You have lied to us. Tell me, why did you not give these brochures to the censor to pass?"

"It was very late," she murmured. "The conference was to begin. We didn't have time."

"Why do you go to other countries so often?"

She answered truthfully. "I serve on fund-raising committees. I visit England and Switzerland to attend meetings. We help Jewish teenagers go to Palestine."

He laughed nastily. "You should have worked much faster and sent out more of your people from Germany where they are not wanted."

"We could not get enough entry certificates from the British Mandate," she stammered.

Now he leaned forward, speaking in clipped, barking tones. "You must not do this. You are giving Germany a bad reputation, taking children from the country. You must stop your work at once. Understand!"

At a hastily arranged conference that night, it was agreed that Eva's usefulness to Youth Aliyah in Germany was at an end. Quickly, before the Gestapo machinery had a chance to list her as a suspicious person, she and Dolph Michaelis applied for a visa to leave Germany for a week to attend a conference in London.

They remained in England for a few months and in 1938 sailed to Palestine.

Shortly before their ship was due to arrive, the Youth Aliyah office received bad news. Eva's father had died in Durham, North Carolina.

Hens Beyth went down to meet the boat with a heavy heart, the joy of meeting his friends dimmed by the sad news he had to tell them.

The travelers had been inoculated against disease, an of-

Eva and Dolph Michaelis

ficial rule for immigrants, and Eva had reacted violently to
the serum. Added to this, the news about her father made
her deathly ill. Henrietta, as usual burdened with an ava-
lanche of work, hastened to see her although she could only
stay a few minutes. "Dolph and I want to be married by a
rabbi," sobbed Eva.

Henrietta soothed her hot forehead. "And so you shall.
We will prepare a lovely wedding."

It was a small wedding, but a wonderful day for the two
who had refused to be parted in spite of dangers. Best of all,
it was a Jewish wedding. They were home.

Afterward, a cousin of Eva's gave a simple reception. As
they sat together drinking tea and eating wedding cake, Henrietta touched Eva on the shoulder. "You must call me Henrietta."

Eva was startled. To Henrietta, as an American, this was not an unusual request to a good friend, but where Eva had grown up, one never used first names except with the most intimate friends. It was unheard of when one of the two people was as respected and famous as Henrietta Szold.

Eva looked into her companion's soft brown eyes, always so full of compassion for others and now so weary, and she saw something else, a deep loneliness. Separated from her loved ones and surrounded by people connected to her only through work, Henrietta yearned for the closeness of someone who loved her.

13

World War II

In 1938, Hitler invaded Austria.

The Germans decided to deport from Hannover, Germany, Polish Jews who had lived there for a number of years. The Polish government, on the other hand, refused to readmit Jews who had been in Germany for more than five years. Those caught in the middle were housed in miserable camps.

In Paris, the son of one of these dispossessed families, Hershl Grynzpan, aged seventeen, assassinated Ernst Vom Rath, Third Secretary of the German Embassy, in Paris on November 7, 1938. On November 9, Hitler and some of his old friends met for dinner in Berlin. Hitler remarked mysteriously that the storm troopers might like to have a little fun that night, and left the dinner early.

There followed a wild night, known as *Kristallnacht*, or "Night of Crystal Glass," because of the sound of breaking glass as Nazi thugs in Berlin ran around breaking the windows of Jewish businesses and desecrating synagogues. Several days later, Hitler met with his top aides. "We must settle the Jewish question once and for all," he said.

Total war was declared against the Jews. Deportation was no longer the answer. The Nazis wanted to exterminate them all.

As the Nazi horde spread over Germany and Austria, threatening other countries as well, like a fungus disease, children would have to be snatched to safety. Fortunately, at last in recognition of the emergency, restrictions on children's certificates were removed by the mandatory government. Now the task was to provide places for them.

In America, Hadassah women started a frenzied drive for funds to take care of the flood of Youth Aliyah youngsters. Henrietta was seventy-eight years old, but the monumental responsibility did not respect age or weariness.

In January 1939, she visited Meier Shefaya children's village and was surrounded by children bringing her gifts of flowers. They knew how precious she was to them and to children not yet rescued. Their spokesman said, "May your days be long, for your task is great and many await salvation through you."

There seemed to be an easing at the start of 1939. Entry certificates were plentiful. The Mufti was in Berlin visiting his pal, Adolf Hitler, so there was no one stirring up the Arabs. Palestine was at peace.

Passover 1939 was an island of happiness for Henrietta. Bertha and Adele had come to Palestine for a visit. Benjamin and Sarah came from their kibbutz for the holiday. It was almost like being home.

But shortly after that, the storm broke.

First, there was a personal blow. Soon after her return home from Palestine, sister Adele fell ill and died quite suddenly. Henrietta was devastated.

The brief honeymoon with British Mandate immigration

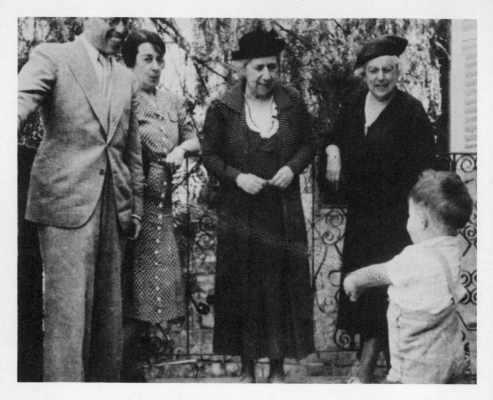

Henrietta with sisters Adele, *left*, and Bertha

officials ended. Great Britain had sent its Prime Minister, Neville Chamberlain, to Berlin to parley with Hitler in an attempt to stave off war. Chamberlain sacrificed part of Czechoslovakia to the Nazis and came home, swinging his furled umbrella and declaring, "We will have peace in our time."

No one believed Chamberlain. You don't make peace with a mad dog by throwing him a bone. The British changed their Prime Minister. The new Prime Minister, Winston Churchill, saw the gathering storm and realized that war was inevitable. The Prime Minister was familiar with the Middle East. He had spent time in Palestine as chairman of the commission that recommended partition. One important point was clear to the round-faced, cigar-chomping Churchill: you don't win a war without oil.

And who had the oil? The Arabs. And what annoyed the Arabs the most? Jewish immigration.

Therefore, at the time when Jews were fleeing for their lives, the British published a new White Paper, limiting severely Jewish immigration into their only haven, Palestine.

For their part, the Nazis also had a plan to dispose of Jews. They devised a "final solution." Certain Jews, and other "undesirables," who were in the concentration camps would be told they were to take showers. But instead of water coming from the pipes, deadly gas would be pumped in. In a few minutes, hundreds of people would be dead. Their bodies would be burned in crematoriums.

The British and French signed a mutual assistance pact with Poland.

On September 1, 1939, Germany invaded Poland. On September 3, 1939, Great Britain and France declared war on Germany.

In October 1939, Eva Michaelis wrote a letter to the Youth Aliyah chairman of Hadassah in the United States: "The lack of additional certificates is presenting us with a grave problem, the terrible problem of the fate of the Jewish children still in greater Germany. It seems quite clear that every boy and girl who will have to remain in Germany during the present regime, or during the war, will be lost to us. It is no longer possible for them to exist there. Even if they go on living, the sufferings and the hardships which they will have to endure will have such a terrible effect on them that it will no doubt be impossible to bring them back to a normal life again."

This was no time to play games with the British. Every Jew who could be saved had to come to Palestine.

And yet, the British were fighting against Hitler.

Zionist leader David Ben-Gurion, who later became Prime Minister of Israel, solved the dilemma neatly: "We will fight the war as if there were no White Paper, and we will fight the White Paper as if there were no war."

As in World War I, thousands of young Jewish Palestinians joined the British army; many of these came from Youth Aliyah.

Henrietta's dream of a beautiful hospital on Mount Scopus had been realized. Ironically, part of its wonderful reputation came from the fact that it was staffed by German refugee doctors, who had been trained in the superb medical schools of Germany and Vienna! When the battle for vital oil shifted the war to North Africa and the Middle East, Hadassah opened its doors and offered the skill of its medical personnel to the healing of wounded and sick British soldiers. Precious medical supplies and equipment came by convoy from America.

During World War I, Palestine had faced terrible problems. There were epidemics and food shortages and great unemployment. In World War II, however, Hadassah was there. It served both the Jewish and Arab populations, inoculating people against diseases caused by food shortages and overcrowding. It also instituted school lunch programs to make sure children were getting at least one good meal a day.

In 1940, with hope for the future, the Alice Seligsberg Vocational School opened, aimed at training young people for useful occupations. In later years, one of the skills the Seligsberg School became known for was fashion design, an entirely different industry for the country.

In the dark of night, the shores of Palestine were patrolled by members of the Haganah, the underground army that had grown from the days of Israel Shohat's Shomrim. Their mission was rescue.

Crouched in the shadows, slipping out of the sight of British army patrols, they scanned the Mediterranean Sea looking for the outlines of boats without lights moving stealthily toward the shore. The boats were any kind of vessel Haganah could obtain, often leaky tubs. They were filled with the desperate, fleeing from Nazi hounds yapping at their heels.

Sometimes the boats sank. Sometimes they were caught by the British and the passengers interned on Cyprus, where at least they were safe.

The lucky ones made it to shore, helped by Haganah patrols and civilians. Quickly, they were brought to homes and camps and absorbed into the rest of the population so the British didn't know they had arrived, at least not officially.

Henrietta was very much opposed to bringing Youth Aliyah children in illegally. She had quite an argument about it with Hans Beyth. Not only did she hate to do anything illegal, but she was afraid that if the British found that Youth Aliyah was flaunting its rules, they'd take away the few certificates now available.

The argument ended with Hans storming from the room. Shortly afterward, Henrietta noticed children in the camps without regular documents. She went to Hans and said apologetically, "Forgive me. I am a foolish old woman. The children must be saved. I will not ask how."

Henrietta's tired heart had begun to fail her and she had to spend periods resting in the hospital. But as soon as she felt strong enough, she was off again, tending to her children.

She longed for home, for "Golden bantam corn and fish with flavor and a walk through the ferny woods," and she turned to the American women of Hadassah, sending them a recorded message:

"I grasp your hand to steady myself. Amid the smoke and din of titanic battle on land, on sea, and in the air, an urgent perspective emerges before my eyes. The forces unloosed, intent upon shattering cherished ideals, shall not achieve their sinister purpose. We are resolved to preserve the essence of our faith and our philosophy while adjusting to new ways demanded by the times and their events. My voice and my words will be followed by the voices and the words of the youth whom you have plucked as brands from the burning to become the builders of the future of Israel in the Land of Israel."

After Henrietta finished speaking, there were greetings from representatives of Youth Aliyah students.

Approximately ten thousand teenagers had been rescued. Henrietta realized that more was at stake than just the physical salvation of young people. She instructed their teachers: "It is for you to heal wounds inflicted by malign cruelty, to replace the wrenches of ties that bound a generation of children to fathers and mothers scattered to the furthest corners of the earth, to restore confidence in men and their works and to encourage aspiration and direct it into channels of action towards culture and peace."

In the midst of all the turmoil, Henrietta had a joy she would never have anticipated. Now when she went to visit Youth Aliyah settlements she received more than flowers. Beautiful chubby babies, grandchildren, were put into her delighted arms.

On her eightieth birthday, December 21, 1940, Henrietta addressed the schoolchildren of Palestine: "In the eighty years I have lived, many wonderful changes have taken place. But in one respect the world has not changed. Today, as long ago, good men and good women do noble acts; today, as long ago, energetic men and energetic women work and achieve; today, as long ago, wise men and wise women think great thoughts. The soul does not change; it only learns to use new and better ways of communicating with other souls. Youth and old age can meet as I am privileged to meet you today with my voice and my soul, and old age and youth can resolve together to live nobly and wisely and energetically."

Although 10,000 young people and children had been rescued by Youth Aliyah, there was sorrow for those who were trapped in Nazi lands and could not be saved. Then, in the fall of 1942, a miracle occurred. A group of 730 children, led by 60 adults, showed up in Tehran, Iran. They had walked across Europe, somehow evading capture, surviving on roots and berries and small animals.

Henrietta, standing at back in center, at her eightieth birthday celebration

In Palestine, the Jews were ecstatic. Although this was but a small group, in comparison with the number who had perished, they seemed to represent a resurrection of the lost. The British mandatory government was sympathetic and quickly granted emergency entry certificates for the group.

But then, a bitter thing happened. The Turkish and Iraqi governments refused to permit passage through their countries. How could the Tehran children get to Palestine? The Jews were stunned at this cruelty.

Three Hadassah women in the United States called on the British ambassador, Lord Halifax, and implored him to use his influence to get the children out. Deeply touched, he said, "It's almost Christmas. How sad it would make me if nothing could be done for wandering lost children at this time of love and caring." He made no promises, but pulled every string he could think of.

Lord Halifax was successful. On January 2, 1943, the chil-

Interviewing one of the Tehran children in Palestine

dren and their escorts, including several people who had
traveled from Palestine to accompany them, left Tehran for
Ahwaz, Iran. They sailed to Karachi, India, and to Bombay
and from there to Port Said, Egypt, from where they came
by train to Palestine. This roundabout journey took seven
weeks. When they arrived, they were greeted with hysterical
joy, their buses pelted with gifts and food as they made their
way across Palestine to their Youth Aliyah camps.

Henrietta knew that there was another side to the story;
children who had suffered so much would have many problems. Many of them were so sick they had to be carried from
the train. Others were wild. They clutched pieces of bread
and hoarded food. They broke windows and would not stay
still. They were often sullen.

They needed a place of peace and quiet, combined with

A Tehran child hands flowers to Henrietta.

patient treatment and gentle firmness. Henrietta established just such a healing place for emotionally wounded children, called Mosad Szold.

The youngest of the Tehran children was a little girl named Sarah, about five years old. She had been hastily added to the group somewhere along the way. It was assumed that she was an orphan.

Little Sarah had suffered so much her body was prey to one illness after another. She was sent to a Youth Aliyah camp where the leader and his wife came to love her dearly. Tenderly, they nursed her back to health. They came to Henrietta with a request: "We would like to adopt Sarah and make her our own little girl."

Henrietta was about to reply that this was a splendid idea, but something stopped her. Somewhere in the chaos of Europe there might be a parent who would claim the little girl. It was a faint chance, but she did not want this fine couple to face giving up their child.

"Wait," she advised them. "You have your own lives to establish. Sarah will be cared for, wherever she goes."

Sarah went to live in a place called Ahawah, near Haifa, where she was the pet of the settlement. Then in June 1944 an amazing thing happened. A cable was received from a man in Russia, signed with his name and the addition "Father of Sarah." The wire read: PLEASE WIRE IMMEDIATELY FATE OF MY DAUGHTER SIX YEARS OLD, BORN IN WILNO, POLAND, EVACUATED FROM MIDDLE ASIA TO HAIFA. WORRIED ABSENCE MESSAGE.

Joyfully, Henrietta cabled to Sarah's father that his little girl was alive and well.

At eighty-three, exhaustion had finally caught up with Henrietta. More and more often, she had to retire to the Hadassah Hospital to rest. But as soon as she found a bit of energy, she was off again, visiting her beloved children.

One evening as she walked through a Youth Aliyah camp,

Henrietta in studio giving radio broadcast in observance of
the tenth anniversary of the Youth Aliyah program

she heard a child crying. She hastened to the little girl and
sat by her bed. "What is the matter, my darling?"

"I want my mummy," the child sobbed. She had the clipped
tones of a well-brought-up English child.

Henrietta stroked her hair. "And where is your mummy?"

The little girl sat up. "You speak English?"

"Of course," said Henrietta. "I'm an American."

They talked together in Henrietta's beloved mother tongue,
English. Little Ilse had been born in Germany and when very
small sent to England for safety. Her parents had apparently
died in a labor camp. In England she was placed with a kind
Christian couple, the only parents she remembered.

"I didn't want to go and be Jewish," said the child. "I just wanted to stay with Mummy and Daddy in England."

Henrietta's heart sank. Dear God, do we have to build a Jewish state over the broken hearts of children? But she could not undo what had been done.

She began to speak. The words came easily in English, and it seemed that she was speaking not only to this one child but to all the children she had rescued. And she was gathering, in this dimly lit bungalow, the whole essence of her life on earth.

"We will keep in touch with Mummy and Daddy," she reassured the child. "After the war, you will be able to visit them. But you see, Ilse, the Jewish people have to survive, to teach others. That's why children like you, standing in for your own parents who did not live, must grow up strong and wise and just.

"There is so much pain in the world, so many people who cannot understand life because they've been hurt or because they have never been taught the truth. It is up to young people like you to build a Jewish state and to show the world how to be strong, yet kind and decent."

Henrietta could no longer travel. Tended by Youth Aliyah girls and devoted Hadassah nurses, she rested in the hospital.

But there was one last job for her. Two of her friends, Chaim Weizmann and Judah Magnes, had quarreled bitterly over politics and become enemies. It happened that they both came to visit her at the same time. She insisted that they clasp hands before her and promise to quarrel no more.

On February 13, 1945, Henrietta Szold died. She was buried on the Mount of Olives. Her son, Simon Kresz, fifteen years old, one of the Tehran children, said the mourner's kaddish.

Afterword

Following World War II, the British gave up the Mandate and left Palestine. The surrounding Arab countries felt they could easily rout the Jews and chase them "into the sea." But the men of the Haganah had trained well. They fought off the invaders in a war called the War of Liberation. Miraculously, in the midst of bitter fighting, on May 14, 1948, the Jewish state of Israel was born, with Chaim Weizmann as its first president.

Hadassah Hospital, as always, cared for the war wounded and the civilian population. On April 15, 1949, Dr. Chaim Yassky, head of Hadassah Hospital, and a convoy of nurses tried to make it up to the besieged building on top of Mount Scopus. They were mowed down by an Arab ambush. The Arabs took possession of Mount Scopus. The great hospital, its nursing school, and Hebrew University stood empty and silent.

Hadassah continued medical activities in makeshift quarters. Determined to build another building, Hadassah members in the United States worked hard to raise the money for the construction. Finally, a new hospital was built at Ein Karem in Jerusalem. Famed artist Marc Chagall designed stained-glass windows depicting the twelve tribes of Israel for the hospital. People come from all over the world to see the beautiful windows.

In 1967, Mount Scopus was liberated and the old Hadassah Hospital opened its doors once more. Now Hadassah's two hospitals care for Jewish and Arab citizens. There is even a radio outreach program that teaches Arabs in other countries about health. The annual inpatient load at the Hadassah hospitals is nearly 50,000, with 550,000 outpatient visits.

Research at the Hadassah hospitals benefits the entire world. Often, American medical people combine their resources with Hadassah doctors and learn from them. The medical school, school of nursing, and dental school, as well as the school of pharmacy, teach first-rate medical practice. They are especially interested in public health.

There are 190,000 graduates of the Youth Aliyah program, who have become leaders of their country. Today, 315 Youth Aliyah installations serve 18,500 boys and girls, many of whom are the children of Jewish people from undeveloped countries who need to learn to live in a modern society.

In addition to Youth Aliyah camps, there are day care centers for disadvantaged youths. The day care centers have Parents' Circles, to which the parents can come in the evening and learn marketable skills. For those children who have had poor educations in their home countries, there is special education to help them catch up. The Hadassah Seligsberg-Brandeis Comprehensive High School, Hadassah Community College, and Hadassah Vocational Guidance Institute teach enriched vocational and academic studies.

Hadassah has always worked with the Jewish National Fund to reclaim the wilderness. Currently, an agricultural

In the Machon Szold Experimental Reading Club for culturally disadvantaged youth, 1977

center is being developed at Kikar S'dom, a desolate area in the Negev Desert. Hadassah Plaza in Bicentennial National Park celebrates the connection between the United States and Israel. Hadassah Tefen, in the upper Galilee, is a modern industrial center.

Hashachar, the Hadassah American youth organization, has 8,000 members, ranging from nine through college age. Hashachar runs Young Judaea summer camps, clubs, leadership training programs, and study-work experiences in Israel.

In March 1987, Hadassah celebrated its seventy-fifth anniversary as part of a year-long celebration. Its membership

A young man works in a vocational shop at Machon Szold, 1977.

of 370,000 women in the United States and Puerto Rico said to one another, "Happy Birthday." Women from all over the world came to Jerusalem for a big celebration. Then, like Henrietta Szold herself, they left the celebrating, rolled up their sleeves, and went back to work.

Index

About the Author

HAZEL KRANTZ has written several other books for young adults. Of this book she reflects, "For many years I had admired Henrietta Szold, not only for her accomplishments, but for her steady sweetness of spirit and for the orderliness, integrity, and compassion she displayed during the arduous years of her service in Palestine. As a wife and mother, I found her fulfillment as the 'mother' to hundreds of boys and girls rescued from the Holocaust very touching. The fact that this occurred after she was sixty years old proves that the gold within us is used even if not in the way we would ordinarily expect."

Ms. Krantz has also taught school and worked as an editor. Presently she is a full-time writer living in Fort Collins, Colorado.